*Jonathan stormed the length of the room
until he stood before Prudence.*

"Miss Beck, look at me and listen. Really listen to what I am saying, because I mean every word and there is nothing. . .I repeat, *nothing* on the face of this earth that will make me change my mind."

He snapped his fingers in front of her face and she blinked. "Prudence Beck, stop denying we're having this conversation. Now listen closely to what I am about to say, and believe it. Believe every word. How dare you use my child to win my acceptance. You have made me realize my neglect and I accept my failure. That can and will be changed. On the other hand, you lied to me regarding everything about yourself, and that cannot be undone." He felt anger build with every word. "You are not trustworthy. You are not honorable. You are not welcome. You are not going to stay. The *Anna Hartwell* should be here in the morning. I want you ready to go on board. . ."

EYES *of the* HEART

Maryn Langer

A Barbour Book

See through the eyes of the world.
See hate, envy, lies.
See through the eyes of the heart
Forgive the sin, love the sinner.

ISBN 1-55748-993-9

Published by Barbour & Company, Inc.
       P.O. Box 719
       Uhrichsville, OH 44683
       http:\\www.barbourbooks.com

Member of the
Evangelical Christian
Publishers Association

Published in the United States of America.

one

On the fourteenth day of January, 1866, in Lowell, Massachusetts, Prudence Beck lied. Not a small white lie to be polite. Not even a medium-sized lie to cover a mistake. In an interview with Asa Mercer, she did the unforgivable—became a party to a Paul Bunyon-sized deceit in her fear-driven desperation to join Mercer's group of quality young women sailing to the Washington Territory.

At the time, however, lying seemed a justifiable means to an end. To Prudence's relief, Mr. Mercer assured her she had indeed answered all the questions satisfactorily and would be a great asset to the Territory. Whereupon, Prudence, with trembling hand, signed a promissory note for the twenty-five dollars required for her fare and clutched the contract Mercer issued guaranteeing her passage.

Into the conversation Mercer skillfully inserted that while some of the women were interested in becoming teachers in the Territory, a goodly number had expressed interest in marriage as well. In the event Prudence had given any thought to matrimony, he, Mercer, had prepared a list of quality men who were also interested in marriage.

Prudence was definitely interested in matrimony and, from the list, she chose "Jonathan Hartwell" because she liked the name. She was handed a letter in which he set forth his expectations. He expected the usual things of a prospective bride. She should be under twenty-five years of age, an able cook who could tend her own garden, an

5

efficient and organized housekeeper, a passable seam-stress. He especially emphasized that she be chaste. At that, Prudence cringed and swallowed.

In her reply to Jonathan Hartwell, which Mercer mailed on a fast packet boat just before his army transport ship, the *Continental,* sailed on the 15th, the only thing Prudence hadn't lied about was her looks. She described herself honestly as Welsh, seventeen hands high, built like a sappling, muddy-water brown hair, forest-green eyes, good teeth, no pox scars.

But the rest of Prudence's letter was a summary of the lies she had told Asa Mercer—lies convincing enough for her to be accepted as a Mercer Belle, and leave Lowell and her hometown of Tyngsboro far behind.

To her credit, however, those falsehoods had not come easily. They were dictated by a despairing woman who feared herself about six weeks pregnant. It was not enough that her beloved husband, Frederick Appleton, had been hanged as a horse thief. She also had learned on the day of his execution that he had three other wives, she being the fourth.

That cold rainy New Year's Day, as she watched Frederick's other wives squabble over which of them should have his body, she had prayed the cobblestones of the Lowell town square might open and swallow her. Despite her fervent pleading, however, the stones remained firmly in place as they had for the better part of a hundred years. Prudence understood she would have to live through the days of heartbreak and humiliation.

She stared at the limp form being cut down from the hanging oak and tried to summon up hate, anger, disgust . . . some emotion. But all she felt was a hollow, cold, numbness where her heart should be. Her only desire was to flee the place where her life had stopped. However, to call as little attention to herself as possible, she moved past the commotion raised by the wives to the entertainment of the crowd.

She couldn't help remembering how she had waited this morning for him to return from his regular five-day circuit as a drummer. And when he did, he came clattering up the street, riding a magnificient chestnut stallion blowing hard. Frederick had ridden fast and long in his haste to be at her side to spend New Year's Day. That's what he had told her and she had had no reason to doubt him. He always spent holidays and Saturdays with her.

Now, her heart wrenched with the knowledge of his whereabouts during those five days each week. She pushed her way through the milling crowd and stumbled blindly in the direction of the small room that was her married home. Once inside, she threw herself across the bed and cried herself out.

Later, much later, she washed her hot, puffy face, drew a straight-backed wooden chair up to the single window where she could see the street. She stared at the nothingness of the soot-smudged brick wall of a neighboring building. It didn't take long for her mind to work up a fine panic over her situation.

Frederick had invested all her savings in a cooperative land purchase and had quickly been cheated of every dime. Today at the hanging she learned that he had invested money from all his wives, so sure was he of the successful outcome of the venture. They, however, all owned homes and land. She was the only one left destitute. Desperate, he had stolen the horse in an attempt to recoup something for her. Unfortunately, he was not experienced in the art of horse thievery. His apprehension was immediate, his appearance in court quick, and justice swift.

Sadly, marriage had meant she could no longer work in the Lowell cotton mill where she had been a well-paid supervisor of the looms. She could think of no way to earn even a meager living.

Several hours later, pride asserted itself and Prudence refused to allow herself to grieve for Frederick beyond the first hot tears. Through the next two weeks, however, it seemed she had a perpetual knot in her throat as she searched desperately for a way to support herself. No one had any sewing, needed their home cleaned, their children tutored, or their bookwork done.

After two weeks of desperate searching, Prudence finally realized her reputation as the fourth wife of Frederick Appleton meant she would never find any but the most lowly work in the worst imaginable places and never rise above it. She would surely starve or die of abuse in Lowell.

She saw no choice but to go home to the little village of Tyngsboro. Home to a weeping, pleading, ineffectual mother and a critical, tight-lipped father. Her two comely younger sisters, who took after their gentle, beautiful mother, had the pick of several counties and chose the handsomest and richest for their husbands. To them their father gave his love and praise and small fortunes for their dowries.

Prudence, on the other hand, looked much like her father and should have been the boy, he said as though it were her fault she wasn't. She could never please him and endured his constant verbal abuse until she was sixteen and able to flee to Lowell and the honest work in the mills.

Her own promised substantial dowry was denied her, because in her father's eyes she, being a Beck, and choosing an Appleton, had married far beneath herself.

Prudence began packing her belongings to return to the cold and hostile home in Tynsgboro when she realized she had missed her second monthly. Her heart stopped. She and her baby would be doomed to a life of disgrace. Her child would carry the stigma for his lifetime. That was when Prudence knelt and prayed through her tears, more earnestly than at any time in her life, for deliverance from such a future.

She wrote a hasty note telling her mother to expect her, and went to post it. There on the wall of the post office was a handbill telling of Asa Mercer and his mission. Prudence never mailed that letter. Instead, she went in haste to see Mr. Mercer.

Thus, came the desperate untruths she wrote to Jonathan Hartwell. And to her mother she mailed a note saying she was going west to Washington Territory to teach school at Hartwell Landing.

The lies tormented Prudence's conscience like a hair vest. All during the trip she had been punished with headaches. The pain had gotten worse and worse the closer to Seattle Mercer's Belles drew. Today, May 29, 1866, more than four months after leaving New York, and only minutes from docking at Seattle and meeting Jonathan Hartwell, she had a headache so blinding she had trouble focusing her eyes.

Prudence pressed her face against the cool glass of the open porthole in her small room and drew a deep breath. The air reeked of the ocean, decaying kelp, and slimy fish, and her unseaworthy stomach turned over. The fog was burning off, drifting away in silvery wisps as the sun rose.

Indeed, every day and night of the journey west she'd had nothing to do besides try out names for the baby, stitching baby clothes by candlelight in the deep of night.

By day, she would watch the water slip past. Night and day she would worry about what Jonathan Hartwell would do when he saw her and learned of her outrageous deception. Now, with the *Tanner* only a few hours away from Seattle, Prudence's nerves were raw, but her thinking infinitely clearer. Why had she ever thought she could get away with such an ungrounded scheme?

One lie would be apparent immediately—the baby. Though the cape she wore made her look like a walking tent, her face, hands, and arms were thin as pencils. She could vividly imagine the man's reaction when presented with both a bride and impending fatherhood.

The second fabrication was Prudence's age. Jonathan Hartwell had been very specific about that. He wanted a young, pliant woman, so Prudence knew beyond a doubt that had she admitted to being thirty-two, two years older than Hartwell himself, he would have concluded she was too long of tooth to learn anything new. Prudence had looked hard in the mirror. Her considerable amount of practical experience would make her a good frontier wife. That should compensate for the deepening parenthesis around her mouth and the crow's feet at the corners of her eyes.

Watching the dock loom nearer and nearer and knowing she would soon have to face the moment of truth, it took every bit of courage Prudence could muster. She adjusted her shapeless dress and covered her condition with a heavy black cloak, set a stylish black bonnet over her plain brown hair pulled back in a braided knot at the base of her neck.

A quick look in the small cloudy mirror above the battered sea chest revealed deep blue smudges which made her eyes look hollow, and because of her constant nausea, her cheeks were sunken and accented with an unhealthy pallor. These added several years to her appearance. Jonathan would need only one quick look to know the truth. Lord help her when he found out. What would he say? "Strumpet, take your baby and pack yourself straight back to Massachusetts."

How, with no money? Prudence's shoulders wilted.

What would she do if Hartwell left her high and dry out here in this wilderness? She pinched the pale cheeks and brought a hint of color to her drawn face. She did look some better. A tiny smile of hope creased her thin cheeks. If women were as scarce as they said, there must be one man starved enough for a good home-cooked meal and a clean house to take in her and her unborn child.

She set her shoulders back and firmed her jaw, though the act jarred her head badly. With determined steps, she mounted the steep narrow stairs to the deck and with each step she searched for some ray of hope, some flaw she might find in Jonathan Hartwell. And then the idea slipped across the threshold of her mind and she gripped it and held it firm. Prudence's head even ached a bit less when it occurred to her that perhaps Jonathan Hartwell had told some lies of his own. She had no guarantee he had been completely truthful with her. Especially when his brother, Ethan, had done the writing and signed as much.

Jonathan's one letter overflowed with details of logging in the Pacific Northwest, the bustling village of Hartwell Landing with over a hundred people now. He told interesting anecdotes about many of the loggers, but it bothered her that he had said so little about himself. Was that because there wasn't much to tell? Suddenly, she doubted it. Everyone had a story and a good one.

Jonathan said he had heard of Washington Territory from Ethan, who rode the circuit there as an itinerant preacher. Then Ethan proceeded to write several more eloquent pages about the territory and it's potential for growth. The letter lavished praise on Asa Mercer for his farsightedness in recognizing the people's need for schools and churches and laws to civilize their towns, and for then having the courage to set in motion some solutions to the problem. Again, she wondered how many of these thoughts were Jonathan's and how many Ethan's.

But when it came to describing himself, Jonathan was far less specific. All he said was that he was from North Carolina, had been in the territory six years, had brown eyes, and that he was bigger than most. About his face, he wrote, "It hasn't yet stopped a clock." Prudence had laughed when she had read that.

Standing on the deck of the fishy-smelling brig as it drew up to the wharf and Seattle, Prudence fervently hoped Jonathan Hartwell had the sense of humor hinted at, for though her condition was not amusing, a light touch could ease the tense moments when he learned the truth about her. As if to reassure her, the baby gave a small kick to let Prudence know she wasn't alone anymore. The little movement brought a glow of warmth to Prudence's heart, but she still quailed at the thought of meeting Jonathan Hartwell.

In an effort to quiet her misgivings, Prudence stood well back from the rail and wondered for the thousandth time what Jonathan would be like. Would he be handsome? Prudence held no illusions about her own looks. Plain as a gunnysack was how her two beautiful sisters described Prudence. She sent her mind scurrying from that thought before what was left of her confidence abandoned her altogether.

What would be the timbre of Jonathan's voice? With his

brother being a preacher, there was a chance Jonathan, too, could have a deep thrilling voice. What bent his disposition? What kind of husband would he be—cruel or kind? Begrudging or generous? Harsh or gentle? Fault finding or forgiving?

Prudence prayed almost constantly for him to possess the last virtue, for what man would not be angry upon learning that his intended wife, besides not being pure, came to him carrying another man's baby. At the thought, Prudence's cheeks burned and her head pounded with renewed fury. Though she loved the little one she was carrying with all her heart, she knew her lie of being chaste was the greatest deceit of all, and the one Jonathan Hartwell would least forgive. It was also the one she could least conceal, and when she pictured the look of rejection on his face, it was the one that made her break into a cold sweat.

two

Pastor Ethan Hartwell had not included his brother, Jonathan, in the scheme to find him a wife. Though Jonathan had returned to the logging camp from Seattle with the news of Asa Mercer's plan to bring women to the territory, it was Ethan who had penned the letter, signed Jonathan's name over his own, and sent it up to Mercer. It was Ethan Hartwell's letter Prudence Beck had answered. Knowing how stubborn his brother could be, Ethan had kept his attempt at matchmaking to himself until the morning Prudence was to arrive. He had let Jonathan read her letter, thinking that would be enough to at least get him to the pier. What happened after that would be up to Prudence. But today Jonathan was not cooperating even a little bit.

Earlier this morning in Jonathan's cabin aboard the *Thomas Hartwell*, the star ship of the Hartwell Lumber Company, Ethan had stood in the doorway and begged Jonathan to reconsider his decision not to meet Prudence Beck. While Ethan had talked, Jonathan polished his razor, returned it to the velvet-lined case, and snapped the lid shut. Eyeing Ethan's reflection in the mirror, he had said, his voice hard and cold, "You had no business butting into my affairs, Ethan. I'm quite able to manage such a mission if I wanted or needed a wife. It is my considered opinion that a woman's always in the way, bossy, demanding. And what happens when she gets pregnant and. . . ."

Jonathan's voice had trailed off into silence, and Ethan

14

knew he was remembering Anna, petite, gentle, helpless Anna brought to a wilderness she couldn't cope with, grew to hate, and died there giving birth to Serena. Ethan had made no mention of Serena in his letter and had felt the sin of his omission weighing heavy on his soul.

"Jonathan, think about Serena. She's growing into a forest creature, not a civilized child. She needs a mother, which means you need to take a wife."

Ethan saw the anger darken the normally soft brown of Jonathan's eyes as he stared into the mirror and raked a large, tortoise-shell comb through thick, sun-streaked brown hair.

"Well, Ethan, I don't want a wife. Losing Anna was a hurt I don't ever want to deal with again. Ever!" He clenched his fist until the knuckles stood white, then carefully laid the comb in the drawer and turned slowly to face his brother. "So I guess you're going to have to be the one to meet Miss Prudence Beck and marry her."

"Jonathan, how many married circuit-riding preachers do you know? Home one night in three months, and that not guaranteed. What woman's going to put up with such treatment? What kind of man would ask her to?"

"Seems plain to me you should have thought of all those things before you set pen to paper and wrote that letter."

"I agree it was a presumptuous thing to do without consulting you. It was ill thought out, a classic example of poor judgment, even if I did and still do have yours and Serena's best interests at heart. I apologize. But Prudence Beck is on the *Tanner* and it's docking later this morning. Are you going to let it come in and have no one there to meet her after she's come all this way?"

The anger faded. Jonathan smiled loftily, and shrugged a carefully laundered white shirt over muscled shoulders.

As he buttoned it, he said, "I don't aim to rescue you from your problem, Brother Ethan. You meet the *Tanner* and the lady gets met. You don't meet her and she's left stranded for about ten minutes until some other fellow sees his chance. Either way, she's going to be taken care of right fine."

Now, while the tailor finished hemming the pants to Ethan's new suit, Ethan stared unseeing at the wake of the arriving ship breaking the blue water of Puget Sound. He grappled with his conscience. A man of God shouldn't be a party to the smallest deception, even if it was with the best of intentions. Whatever had possessed him to do such a thing? Jonathan was right. He could get a wife if he chose, but Jonathan was too bullheaded to know he needed one.

"That'll be a quarter," the tailor said as he straightened, his knees cracking from the years of ups and downs.

Ethan blinked at the amount, but with the *Tanner* approaching the dock, he didn't have time to dicker the price.

Prudence's first sight of Seattle made her doubt the wisdom of her decision to join Asa Mercer's group. Never had she seen a more unappealing town than this scattering of shacks that clutched the sides of steep hills and crouched along the waterfront, all huddled together under a cold, drizzle of rain. She wished she were invisible. Not only was her head pounding, but now her stomach hurt. Her hand balled into a fist and pressed into the pain. It brought no relief and Prudence wished she could die. If the Lord struck her down at this moment, it would be such a comfort. She'd get on with paying for her sins, whatever He asked of her, and sometime in the far-off future she might earn His forgiveness.

Asa Mercer concluded his conference with the captain of the *Tanner* and stepped onto the deck. "Ladies, I must speak a few words with you before we dock," he said. "I have repeated this many times during our months together, but it needs to be reinforced this one last time. Every man in Seattle and along the Puget Sound is here to meet our boat. Most haven't been in the company of a lady for a very long time. Those of you who did not select a name from the list I presented you and thus guarantee yourself a gentleman to meet you, please hold yourselves aloof and choose wisely. There are many here who are not worthy of your high quality and will make you most unhappy." He dipped his hat to his charges. "Now, I intend to talk to the men before any of you steps a single foot ashore."

The excited crowd on shore snatched up the lines thrown from the *Tanner* and the brig was snubbed to the dock in record time. Asa Mercer had a fine voice and he quickly had the attention of the eager men. "Gentlemen, I want you to know that I arrive here with women of the highest quality. They are not leaping off this boat, into your arms, and saying marriage vows all within the space of an hour. Though, upon seeing preacher Ethan Hartwell in your midst and him decked out in a fine new suit, I have concluded that is the plan many of you have."

Ethan, at the mention of his name, raised his hand in a friendly salute. Prudence heard no more of Mercer's speech, so intent was she upon studying the preacher. He was loose-limbed, frail-looking, and the traditional long-tailed black coat that marked him as a man of God accented his rounded shoulders. Only the lower half of his sun-darkened face showed beneath the wide brim of the black slouch hat until he removed it and revealed a remarkable mane of red hair. It was thick and combed back, falling in a loose cascade over the collar of his coat.

"If you want the preacher's services, get behind me," someone shouted. The crowd began to swirl into an uneven line around the Reverend Hartwell, pinning him against tall piling. He was hidden from Prudence's view and there was no way she could make herself known. She also knew he was not going to be seeking her for awhile.

At this moment the rain stopped and sunshine broke open the clouds for a couple of hours.

It was late in the afternoon when Ethan finished marrying the last couple. Prudence watched the scene on the dock from the shadow of the bulkhead and, as the day lengthened, felt the knot of pain in the core of her head tighten and writhe. All afternoon she had searched the faces that ebbed and flowed along the wharf and she had yet to find one she thought fit Jonathan Hartwell, especially if he looked anything like his brother.

For Amos Sperry, captain of the *Tanner*, the trip had been a disappointment. Sperry, short and round, with a gray beard and a hearty laugh, loved to mingle with his passengers, particularly the pretty, single women. From the first time he met Prudence when she boarded his ship in San Francisco, he had liked her and had looked forward to her company on the voyage. But he soon realized she was more withdrawn and uncommunicative than any woman he had ever known. The sad aura around her and her obvious seasickness soon doused any spark of romantic interest. She did thank him gratefully for his efforts to make her barren little cabin more comfortable, and he felt a growing fatherly protectiveness for the painfully thin figure always hiding inside the full black cape.

It caught at his heart to hear her soft, "Dear Father in Heaven," as she got a closer view of Seattle. Now, she stood all alone on the deck, looking more pale and frightened than at any time on the trip. He walked up beside her and gruffly made his offer. "In a few days, after we've unloaded the cargo, we'll be turning back south again." He gestured toward a ship tied alongside the dock. "That ship is here from Jonathan Hartwell's mill, loaded with lumber for us to take to San Francisco." He cleared his throat nervously. "This is wild country up here, not for everyone. What I'm trying to say to ye, ma'am, is that I'll give ye passage back to San Francisco, if you've a mind for it." He accented the word 'give'. "I have friends. We'd get ye passage back East and home."

He peered carefully at her pale lips, watched her attempt to be unobtrusive as her fisted hand disappeared inside the cape.

For a moment Prudence was tempted—Puget Sound looked like such a dreary uncivilized place, and she was alone. The girls she had traveled with for four months were gone from the ship. Most had already found and married their intended grooms. Canoes and rowboats still bobbed on the water of starboard as their mackinaw-clad, full-bearded occupants hovered about the ship and dock, shouting coarse enticements to those few women awaiting transportation to boarding houses. None seemed to pay any mind to the steadily falling rain when the reward for patience was a glimpse of a fashionable young woman from the East. Prudence was touched by the captain's offer of deliverance from the wilderness. But the image of the righteous faces of Tyngsboro matrons looking first at her and then at her baby and clucking their disdain loomed huge in her mind. Her voice was firm. "Thank you for your generous offer, Captain, but, no, I've made a committment to a gentleman here." Quite suddenly a little chuckle spilled out despite her worries. "And I wasn't born for the sea, that's very clear. The muddy ground of Puget Sound will suit me better than the roll of the finest ship."

The captain nodded and commandeered a deckhand to help with Prudence's baggage while he gripped her elbow. "Come along, then. Ye've got to face the music some time. Hidin' here won't get ye the husband ye came for nor a room for the night," he said as he steered her down the gangplank. "A desperate lot ye ladies are, victims of that terrible tragic war just finished. Left with no choice but seekin' men a continent away," he growled and spit angrily into the harbor. "It's glad I am there's good men here for ye." He flapped an impatient hand in the direction of the thinning crowd. "But if you don't hurry, all that'll be left are the disillusioned drunks. The worthy ones will be gone back to their axes and you'll be outta luck." He dropped her elbow. "I wish ye well." He turned on his heel, hailing a fellow captain. Together they disappeared into the milling throng toward a wharfside saloon.

The deckhand sent Prudence a look of sympathy as he stacked her cases and boxes on the dock. Prudence's body still rocked with the rhythm of the sea, and she closed her eyes to steady herself. She glasped her hands tightly and offered up a prayer. *Dear Father in heaven, I am so frightened and need Your comfort and guidance as never before in my life. I beseech Your spirit to be with me as I face the unknown. Amen.* Her words seemed to rise and become trapped inside the unfurled sails of the *Tanner* now pulling lazily against her moorings. Uncomforted, resolutely, she opened her eyes. She took a deep breath that did nothing whatever for the pain in her head or the ache that continued to gnaw viciously at the pit of her stomach.

Finished with his last marriage ceremony, Ethan Hartwell came forward to where Prudence stood. She tucked a stray lock up under her bonnet, smoothed her cape past her thickening waist and gave her skirt a useless fluff. With fingers made clumsy by dread, she checked to be sure her cloak was fully buttoned.

The Reverend Hartwell raised his hat in greeting. "I do hope you're Miss Prudence Beck." His voice rolled like distant summer thunder, deep and penetrating.

"I am, sir." Somehow she managed to sound normal, though her heart pounded like it was trying to escape from her rib cage. But even as she stretched out her hand to the Reverend Ethan Hartwell in greeting, her eyes seemed to have a will of their own and continued to scan the remaining male faces for that of Jonathan Hartwell.

Then Prudence saw a man appear on a rise a few feet from where she and Ethan exchanged pleasantries. Tall, distinguished, he stood quietly, his stance that of a sea captain bringing his ship into port.

He was dressed in the latest eastern fashion, but his tanned skin and the sun streaks in his heavy brown hair revealed he did not spend his days in frivolous dalliances. The fine broadcloth suit accented his lean muscled body. But it was his eyes that held her captive. They were like none other she had ever known—deep-set under thick dark brows, and burning with a disquieting energy. They regarded her intently from a face lined and harsh, did not look at any of the other women, just her.

Her heart continued to beat furiously, and for a second her surroundings blurred. Was this magnificient creature Jonathan Hartwell? Most certainly not. This man would not need his brother to write a letter in search of a wife. All he need do was crook a finger and half the women of the Territory would be at his feet. At the ridiculous image of an endless carpet of obeisant woman, Prudence's heart steadied, her breathing slowed. She was surely mistaken about the man's being Jonathan Hartwell. This man wasn't particularly interested in her. It was someone else he was watching for. That's what she told herself.

"I felt it prudent to wait to disembark until you had done with your official business," Prudence heard herself saying. "I had no idea you would be called upon to perform marriages immediately upon our arrival. What happened to Mr. Mercer's plans for proper boarding houses and chaperoned courting?"

Ethan Hartwell smiled a wide, friendly smile. "Yes, well, Asa forgot to consider the distances from Seattle to where many of these men live and work. For them courting here would be impossible. Guess they decided it wasn't safe to leave fine single women waiting unattended in the city. Most figured they'd marry now and court later." He looked out over couples already beginning to load their wagons and hoist luggage up gangplanks of lumber packets. "Can't say as I blame them." Then, shifting uneasily from one foot to the other, his eyes scanned the harbor.

Prudence followed his gaze until it came to rest on the newly painted, full-rigged lumber packet moored nearby. Nets filled with lumber were rising from its main hold and disappearing inside the *Tanner*. "If you'll allow me, I'll happily see to the transfer of your things to the *Thomas Hartwell* riding at anchor yonder." He pointed to the ship a couple of berths away.

Ethan did not mentioned Jonathan or his failure to appear, and Prudence sensed all was not well between the brothers. "Will your brother, Jonathan, be aboard?"

"I doubt Jonathan is back from seeing to his business. The exchange of lumber for supplies and the remaining cash sometimes takes an enormous amount of haggling until both parties are reasonably satisfied. Jonathan is a shrewd bargainer, so negotiating takes time." Ethan spoke easily enough, but his cheeks reddened and he ran his index finger around his collar.

Busying himself, he gathered her baggage, leaving only a small carpetbag. As she bent to retrieve it, her eyes were pulled again to the rise. He was still there. She could not deny it. He watched her every move. She started to ask Ethan if the man on the hill were perchance Jonathan, but before she could form any words, he left the rise without a backward glance and disappeared into the crowd.

three

From a knoll rising steeply above the waterfront, Jonathan Hartwell stood, and with a practiced eye he studied the newly arrived Mercer's belles. They came in all sizes, shapes and ages and were snapped up as fast as they set foot off the *Tanner*. All except one. Tall, haggard-looking, dressed for mourning with a full cape over her thin shoulders and an unbecoming black bonnet, she stood like a statue on the wharf. Repeatedly, his eyes has been drawn to her. At last, she looked his way, then self-consciously she quickly shifted her attention to the collection of bobbing boats that swarmed around the *Tanner* like bees around apple blossoms.

Jonathan pretended he hadn't seen her, whirled, and stalked down the hill and turned toward the counting house where the lumber sales were cleared. He could cheerfully wring the neck of that meddling brother of his. What on earth or heaven had possessed Ethan to send for a bride without discussing it first? Just because he was educated and a minister didn't mean he could read people's minds and hearts and know better than the person what was best.

Ethan had no right to humiliate him like this! All of Seattle—all of Puget Sound knew there was a bride for him on that ship, a bride *he* had learned about only this morning. He was a full-grown man, thirty years old, capable of running a highly successful business. And, if the present specimen were any example, he had considerable more ability than Ethan in selecting a wife.

Jonathan tried to remember when he'd felt this angry. Years ago, maybe as long as five years ago when Anna had died and their baby had lived. Her life for Serena's. Then, as now, he had felt helpless, at the mercy of others, and this had only served to increase his fury. There were hundreds more churning thoughts seething for release, but Jonathan had long been taught by a stolid, even-tempered father to keep his rage controlled. He must keep his head as he bargained for the best price for their lumber. He would put her out of his mind, keep his mind on business, and when they had to meet, he would be civil but no more. Then, send her back where she came from as soon as arrangements could be made.

Having resolved how to handle the problem of Prudence Beck, Jonathan stepped into the trading office and let business fill his thoughts. However, from his chair he could see the deck of the *Thomas Hartwell* and he couldn't keep his eyes from glancing out the window more often than he was wont to admit.

Aboard the *Thomas Hartwell*, Ethan led Prudence Beck down a flight of stairs and deposited her cases inside a scrupulously clean, but cramped cabin. "Not fancy, I fear," he said as he set her cases on the floor. "Sailors don't much care as long as they have a place to sleep."

The odor of lye almost choked Prudence as she stepped into the cabin. "Thank you, sir, for bringing me aboard. There won't be a problem if I open the porthole, will there?" she asked as she stepped over the luggage on the way to fresh air.

"No, I suppose not. A bit close in here, I'll admit."

Prudence hung her head out the porthole and filled her lungs. Feeling substantially better, she turned back to find Ethan framed in the doorway, his face twisted with worry.

"Are you feeling unwell?"

"I'm much better now, thank you."

"If there is anything you need, ask anyone close. The men will be happy to serve you."

"Thank you, Pastor Hartwell." She paused, wondering how she was going to say this without appearing unduly anxious.

"Oh, Ethan. Please call me Ethan." She nodded, cleared her throat and began. "I don't want to appear eager, but have you any idea when Jonathan will be coming aboard? I'm looking forward to meeting him."

"Uh, yes...well. I doubt he'll be here anytime soon. I wouldn't wait up for him. His mood is sometimes not cheerful after these lengthy bargaining sessions. If he feels he's been taken advantage of, it takes him several days to regain his normal good humor." Unconsciously, Ethan began wringing his hands. "Please be patient with him, Prudence. Jonathan has been a widower for almost five years and he is running skittish about remarrying."

Alarm sent Prudence's heart racing. "Ethan, you didn't tell Jonathan you were writing that letter, did you?" she blurted out.

Ethan blushed and ran his forefinger around his collar. "I must confess, I took a bit of liberty."

Prudence unconsciously took a step back and gaped at Ethan. "A bit of liberty?" She fought the urge to shake her finger in his mottled face and scream at him. "I do think you weren't quite fair with either of us," she said evenly.

Ethan cleared his throat and set his hat more firmly on his head. "Jonathan and I discussed my breach of conduct this morning and I agree with both of you that I did overstep my bounds. I apologize to you for leading you to erroneous conclusions, but it was done out of love and and with the best of intentions, I assure you. I have an enormous concern over Jonathan's great need."

"What need would be great enough for a man of the cloth to commit such a large and deliberate deceit?"

"The need of a lonely little girl for a kind and loving mother, and the need of a man growing bitter and hard from grief, for an understanding and caring helpmate." He bowed his head. "I did what I did out of love for them both. But, sadly, I forgot to think about the recipient of that letter."

Prudence's own thoughts tumbled and her lips twisted into a wry smile. At least she wasn't the only one who hadn't told the full truth. While that fact didn't absolve her sin, at least she had good company.

Ethan raised tortured red-rimmed eyes to meet Prudence's faltering gaze, and she knew she had to tell him of her own deceits. She twisted the strings of her reticule around her fingers as she built her courage. "I, too, have a confession to make," she said. "However, what I have done is far worse than what you did." Her voice faded to a whisper and Ethan stepped closer.

Prudence squared her shoulders and forced herself to look squarely at Ethan while she told him her story.

He removed his hat, shook his head and, with a firm grip on the brim, turned his battered black hat in slow circles. At last, he said, "We are a pair, you and I. Interesting the lengths desperate people will go in trying to solve their problems." He crossed the remaining distance until he stood next to Prudence. "You're a brave lady to take such risks for a respectable life for yourself and your child. One day Jonathan will appreciate the great courage it has taken for you to travel alone to the Washington Territory. However, I think it would be wise to keep your reasons between the two of us for now."

Prudence couldn't agree more. Unfortunately, it would be impossible to keep her secret hidden too much longer. *Please, dear Father, help me*, was all she could think to pray before she dissolved into tears.

Ethan placed a comforting arm around her shaking shoulders. "I know Serena will love you immediately and I have great faith that your gentle hand will bring Jonathan to the altar and quickly, too," he said.

Fumbling through the depths of her handbag, Prudence produced a white handkerchief and brushed away the tears. "I shall pray it is so and I would appreciate your prayers, also."

"You and Jonathan already have them. This next six weeks is going to be difficult tracking for you both."

"I have no idea how to tell my story so that he will understand and forgive me."

Ethan replaced his hat and made his way through the cases to the doorway. "One day Jonathan will come to you and when he does, you will know what to say and do." He gave her a wide smile of encouragement. "I wish I could travel with you tomorrow, but I must remain in Seattle for meetings and then ride my circuit. I usually return to Hartwell Landing in time to celebrate the Fourth of July. That's a very special day at the Landing. Serena's birthday."

Prudence watched the nervous twitching of Ethan's slender fingers along the brim of his hat. "May the Lord travel with you, Ethan, and bring you safely home."

The dark waters of the Puget Sound hissed past the low quarter-decked schooner like the vicious gossip of toothless crones. Prudence stood at the ship's rail, the fine spray from the white foam dewing her cheeks. Unable to sleep for her roiling emotions, anticipation mingled with dread, she had been standing like this since an hour before dawn, long before they were scheduled to dock at Hartwell Landing.

Since stepping aboard the *Thomas Hartwell,* Prudence had spent as little time as possible below in her assigned cabin. She didn't want to miss a moment of the wonder of this new land, the beginning of her new life. However, while she prayed it was a new beginning, she constantly fought the fear that before Jonathan Hartwell came to know her at all, he would reject her and send her packing.

Low, sullen clouds filled the night sky and denied a glimpse of moon or of any other heavenly body. Now with the coming of daylight, rain and fog hid sky and land. Still, Prudence sensed the land's vast mysterious presence, detected its breath, the snow-cooled breeze from the mountains whispering through the evergreen trees, their fragrance spinning through the air currents that swirled around the fully loaded schooner.

Prudence Beck liked the feel and smell of the land and the sea. She liked the untamed rawness. It was clean and untouched, free of judgment and hypocrisy. Here, a person could be his own best self. This place suited her.

Suddenly, through a brief window in the fog, Prudence could see the shore. The ship was sailing directly toward land. It was her cry that brought Jonathan Hartwell struggling into a yellow sou'wester as he came charging up the companionway from his stern quarters.

Jonathan, upon reaching the deck, raced up to where the first mate stood at the wheel. Fog swirled dense arms in battle with the wind and lost. The ship, its sails close-hauled, rode smoothly through the rough water. A quick

look at the compass. They were right on course. Jonathan
sniffed the air. The musky smell of land overpowered the
salt smell of the sea. They were nearing the end of the
Sound and here where the land mass outweighed that of the
water, the wind changed direction and with half gale force
blew out to sea. He could detect nothing amiss. Why had
she screamed?

He marched over to where she stood. "What did you
find that required a scream bloodcurdling enough to wake
the dead?" he roared over the wind and the sea.

Prudence, her chin high, backed away from his anger.
She had seen what she had seen. It wasn't her fault the
lookout and the wheelman were visiting. "The fog lifted
but a moment and I saw clearly the ship was sailing toward
a point of land that stuck out into the channel."

Prudence, she scolded herself, when will you learn to be
gentle? She dropped her eyes and persuaded a slight blush
into her cheeks. "I do feel foolish now, however, since I
seem to be the only one who saw it. I apologize for waking
you needlessly." She hoped that was humble enough to
appease him. Going crosswise of his disposition before
breakfast wasn't the way to win his heart.

Jonathan harrumphed. "You're tired and jumpy. A
good rest when we get to Hartwell Landing will set you
right." He studied the passing terrain. The ship was well
in the channel and sailing fine. He turned and looked hard
at Prudence and wondered about her skittishness.

This was Prudence's first close-up look at Jonathan and
she studied him intently. He was the man on the rise in
Seattle. She was positive of it.

Freshly awakened, the thick sun-streaked mane of his
hair tangled about his head as the wind whipped around his
ears. Beneath the smooth darkly tanned skin, his cheeks

were still lightly flushed with sleep. His eyes were clear, the whites contrasting sharply against the iris, deep brown made tawny by shades of gold, as if dusky forest light were drifting in them. Even in this moment of distraction and confusion, Prudence shivered in wonder at the sheer physical presence of the man—a sense of power and arrogance that at the same time both repelled and attracted her intensely.

Free of fog, the sky and sea blended into an unbroken gray, save for the whitecaps churning from the water. The heavily laden ship rode low in the water and, as the bow plowed into the rising waves of the incoming tide, a heavy mist sprayed the deck. Jonathan was aware that Prudence was becoming more damp with each new wave. Yet she clenched the railing with both hands and showed no sign of coming to her senses and seeking shelter. At this rate she would be down sick for sure, and he didn't have time for that. Until he could make arrangements for her departure back to civilization, he wanted her healthy.

"Get below before you're drenched," he ordered.

Prudence felt her dander rise again. His bossiness made being sweet and gentle extremely difficult. Still. . . there was a great deal at stake, so she swallowed the hot words burning her tongue. Instead, she smiled and tilted her head as she had watched her sisters do when they wheedled their way into or out of something. "If I'm not in the way, I'd prefer staying up top. The cabin is so stuffy and I'm not a good sailor."

Jonathan let his eyes run over her. The woman must have on a dozen layers of clothing and the wetter they got, the heavier they would become. Soon she'd be lucky to stand upright. Yet, he understood her reluctance. Her cabin was stuffy and smelled strongly of lye from the repeated scrubbings he had insisted on before he left for Seattle. But fearing she might misinterpret any conciliatory words, he decided against letting her know of his sympathy.

He kept his voice purposely rough with an edge of irritation. "A tarpaulin for Miss Beck, then," he said to a deck hand hovering nearby.

A tarpaulin was brought. Fastened round Prudence's shoulders, it hung down to the deck and she looked like a candle snuffer. The wind quickened and pulled at the satin ties of her bonnet, loosening them. Just as the wind lifted the bonnet from her head she managed to free a hand and snatch the hat, drawing it inside the tarpaulin. Instantly, the brisk wind swept her hair into streamers. Fighting in vain to tame the flowing tresses back into a knot, she gave up with a shrug and turned into the wind. With a shake of her head, she set her whole mane of brown hair flying in the gale. Her cheeks flushed and her eyes sparkled.

Jonathan's heart accelerated and for the briefest of moments he yearned to hold her in his arms. *You're getting daft, my man. Too many days and nights alone in the woods. Got to hurry and get my fortune made and take Serena and me off to San Francisco where I can find her a proper mother.*

Prudence felt his eyes on her and she turned to find him standing mid-deck, his hands on his hips, staring at her. In his haste he had not snapped shut his sou'wester. It flapped open, revealing a white linen shirt, slipped over his head and stuffed hastily into his breeches. The skin of his chest was tanned and the hair upon it was thick and golden brown, tight whorls filling the vee of his shirt. She blushed at so revealing a sight and, lest he read the vulnerability in her eyes, quickly turned her head to regain control of her undisciplined emotions.

When she looked again she found he stood by her side, gripping the teak rail, peering through the rapidly dissipating fog. "We should still be an hour away from home," he said. Yet there onshore was a prominent sign declaring the large wharf as property of Hartwell Lumber Company. A number of crude buildings hugged the shore and they were sailing past them all. Jonathan whirled to call out his orders in a low but penetrating tone which seemed to carry to every corner of the ship.

"Stand by to go about!"

"Stand by to go about!" The echoing roar of the mate's scattered the crew to their duties.

The tackle screamed through the blocks, and the yards creaked and crackled under the weight of the sails. In the wind holding steady at half a gale, the canvas flagged and then filled again with a sound like the falling crash of a giant fir.

Prudence watched Jonathan as he conned his ship around so that the land swung across the bow. The deck lifted at a sharp angle beneath their feet and the lumber packet began a wide arc. He nodded his satisfaction and returned his attention to Prudence.

She blushed to her hair roots as she realized she had been inspecting each feature of his face. It was square-set and lean like the rest of him, with eyes that looked like he worked hard to keep the expression from them. He didn't smile, but his mouth widened. The upper lip was rounded and had two definite peaks. She liked that. And his square chin had a deep cleft. She liked that best of all. However, he and Ethan looked and acted nothing alike. If she hadn't been told, she would never have guessed they were brothers.

Jonathan took in Prudence encased in unattractive widow's weeds and a black cloak which covered her dress from her throat to somewhere in the vicinity of her knees. He wondered if she were another victim of the War trying to put her life back together. If she was, she wasn't going to do it at his expense. Still. . . her face might have been pretty if it weren't so thin and pale. Maybe it was her hair, light brown with gold lights, and flying around like whipping spring willows, that made her look old. He took her for at least thirty, but thought when she smiled it took five years off her.

Under his intense perusal it took all her resolve not to flee wordlessly to her cabin. Knowing what was at stake, however, she forced herself to stand quietly, a hand resting on her stomach and her eyes fixed on his face.

"I. . .I. . .I'm not exactly what you said you wanted in a wife," she began, giving no clue that she knew he hadn't written the letter. "But I came anyway. I keep hoping you'll overlook what I am not until I can show you what I am."

"I didn't say I wanted a wife. That idea was all brother Ethan's. I couldn't very well leave you alone in Seattle, but I only brought you down here because, on such short notice, I couldn't find a proper ship going to San Francisco. However, as soon as one comes to Seattle I've left word to be notified. If my lumber schooner returns from San Francisco before I hear, we'll send you down when we get it loaded. The accommodations won't be first-class, but they're decent and safe."

"How long will that be, do you think?"

"This time of year, ships come and go every week or so and my schooner is due within the next two weeks. My advice. . .don't unpack and settle in. It won't be worth your time."

"Thank you for the warning." *All this way and this is my welcome to Hartwell Landing.* She ·wanted to cry, but instead, she forced a smile and turned her eyes landward to watch the long wooden wharf grow slowly larger.

Prudence would not let him know how badly he had hurt her. She composed her face into an unemotional mask, and said in crisp, business-like tones, "It appears we are soon to dock. I had best look to my cases." She gave him a curt nod and made her way with uneven steps across the rolling deck and down the stairs to her little cabin in the stern.

Safely inside and the door shut, she waited to be overwhelmed by a flood of tears, to feel completely helpless and distraught by the situation in which she found herself.

Instead, when she thought of Jonathan, she was confused by the contraction in her lungs that left her breathless, a remarkable warmth of her cheeks and the skin of her throat, a prickling of the fine hairs at the nape of her neck, and a dryness of her mouth. Why did she feel these things when he had rejected her so completely?

Honestly, Prudence, I don't understand you. Get hold of yourself. But the lecture did nothing to help her control the unfamiliar feelings. Jonathan Hartwell seemed totally lacking that kind of sensitivity or any of the compassion she had so admired in Frederick. Yet, she found him unaccountably attractive. She cradled her still-burning cheeks in the palms of her hands, breathed deeply to open her lungs, and prayed for an immediate return of the proper sense of decorum and emotional control.

After removing the tarpaulin, Prudence hung her damp bonnet on a hook to dry and patiently brushed the tangles from her hair, fastening the strands in a proper knot. She stood at the open porthole and watched as the lumber packet toiled toward the dock at the Hartwell lumber camp. Leaden clouds hid the tops of the tall pines and firs, and cold unyielding rain began.

Prudence, worn from her many sleepless nights and constant bouts with seasickness, fought hard against the depression threatening to engulf her and refused to surrender. She must go on having faith that all would be well. She had no other choice. She pinched her cheeks into bloom, determinedly set a pleasant smile, closed her tapestry carpetbag, and climbed the stairs to the deck.

The lumber packet seemed not to be drawing closer to Hartwell Landing, though animated clusters of loggers materialized out of nowhere, pointing and gesturing toward the ship.

Prudence then noticed a lugger, a small fishing boat, raising sails and coming out from the wharf to meet the packet.

Jonathan appeared at her elbow, and she jumped, startled from her thoughts. "With the load the ship's carrying she doesn't respond well to the wheel," he said. "The water's too rough right now to chance docking. You're welcome to stay aboard until the seas calm."

Prudence held firmly to the large twist of hair at the base of her neck while the wind flapped her full skirt around her legs like a flag. Slowly, she turned to face him. Her eyes were green, a deep green like the hemlock, but Jonathan had the feeling if the sun had been shining her eyes would have reflected the light and become more emerald. *Jonathan, why do you care in the slightest what color her eyes are or would be? Better keep your mind hard on what's important, that's what you'd better do.*

Prudence forced herself to smile at him. "If I have a choice, Captain Hartwell, I would much prefer going ashore at the first opportunity," she replied.

"You'll be wet and cold," Jonathan said. "The lugger sails will be close-hauled, and with this wind, it will be a rough passage."

"I'm sure it will be, but it will soon be over and I shall be on solid ground permanently. You have no idea how I have prayed for that possibility over the past months," said Prudence. He straightened and looked down on her from this close proximity. She was more than a little aware of his height. How well the two of them fit together. But what did that matter? He didn't want her here, and once he learned the full truth, he wouldn't wait for a proper ship to San Francisco. He would ship her to anywhere on the first thing he could find that floated.

"You have been duly warned, Miss Beck. I shall not be sympathetic to your condition should you fall ill during the crossing."

With that parting volley, Jonathan disappeared and soon returned with a couple of sailors, handkerchiefs bound about their heads and earrings in their ears, their faces burned by the winds and pickled by the salt until the skin had turned a permanent mahogany brown.

"Please see that Miss Beck is safely aboard the lugger," Jonathan ordered. Then, he turned back to her. "Your sea chests and cases will have to wait until we can dock the ship. I hope that won't be too much of an inconvenience."

His voice didn't sound as though he much cared if it were an inconvenience or not, but Prudence chose to ignore that fact. Instead, she answered in her sweetest manner, "I'm grateful to be allowed to go ashore, Captain Hartwell. I ask nothing more than that, thank you."

Jonathan's eyes darted everywhere but on her as he jumped from the ship into the lugger and received her stiff-armed when she passed from the steadying hands of the two sailors. "You'll be more comfortable seated in the cabin, Miss Beck. It's going to be a wet run over to the dock."

Prudence again turned pleading eyes toward him. "I'd rather take my chances with the sea than go inside." She stood, head bowed in deference, waiting for his answer.

He shrugged and set his mouth in a thin line. "Very well," he said and reached for a tarpaulin and again fastened it around her shoulders. "This won't help much, but a little protection's better than none at all."

"Thank you," she said softly, and handed her carpetbag to a seaman.

Jonathan pretended not to hear, pulled the tiller tight against his hip and bellowed, "Cast off, there! Hands to the halyard!" The two sailors strained at the tackle and the lugger leaped away from the lumber packet.

"Lively with that sheet, now!"

Jonathan hauled the tiller over, and the lugger dashed forward, as handy as a horse in the hands of a skillful rider. Even in sheltered Puget Sound, there was enough of a sea running to make the lugger lively as she met it.

Riding the motion of the sprightly little boat, Prudence held on with all her might and found herself swaying easily in rhythm with the boat's quick motions. She had not done that, not once in the long sea journey. Suddenly, she realized this was the moment when she should be desperately seasick. It was interesting that nothing of the sort was happening. Prudence noticed with deep amazement that the buildings of the camp showed up above the dock, and then disappeared as the lugger stood up on her stern and dove into the trough. None of this caused Prudence a single qualm. She was perfectly at ease.

With the lugger sailing well, Jonathan turned his attention to Prudence. Though she clutched the rail in a death grip, she seemed obviously quite comfortable inside. "I thought you said you were a poor sailor," he said to her. "Was that to drum up sympathy?"

Prudence smiled at him. "If it were sympathy I wanted, I would certainly try a different tack than fiegning seasickness. I've just been puzzling over my feeling of well-being. I haven't felt this comfortable since I began my ocean journey from the east. I truly have no explanation."

"It's good you are feeling well. You'll make a much better impression on the camp if you're not green around the gills when you arrive." With that observation, Jonathan turned from her.

Why does he care if I make a good impression? She would think more on that later.

Jonathan bellowed to the seaman, "Stand by to go about!" The lugger came up into the wind, her canvas volleying, and then she shot into the lee of a larger fishing boat riding her anchor at the wharf. The little fishing vessel surged beside the wharf, the decking level with Jonathan's shoulder and beneath him boiling green water. This was a nervous moment as he held the tiller and watched the hausers fly into the waiting hands on the dock. Quickly, the lugger was snubbed tight and the plank secured.

Prudence let fall the tarpaulin, tucked her hair into the remnant of a knot, and wished she had her bonnet to cover the disarray of her hair. She did so want to make her entrance with some dignity.

Jonathan tested the ropes, then leapt up onto the plank.

He reached for Prudence's hand, which she placed on his large open palm and watched as he closed his fingers over it.

"Step up now," he said. "Place your foot carefully lest it catch a crack and spin you into the water." He looked down. "Spin us both into the water."

Prudence nodded her understanding, stepped carefully up onto the gangplank and moved slowly along the swinging walkway. When she was close enough, Jonathan let go and other hands reached out to assist her. Safely on the wharf, she stood among the men, assorted in ages from dewy cheeked lads to bewhiskered old tars. They came in sizes from many who were shorter than she to a few who were enormous and loomed over her. They were all dressed in freshly laundered flannel shirts and work pants.

They all had one goal—a long look at Prudence. At the moment they cared not whether she was young or old, fair or not. That would be discussed later. She was female, and nothing was more important than that in this place where single women seldom came.

Acutely embarrassed, Prudence drew her cloak tightly under her chin and held the hem against the brisk breeze. She would have been frightened, except that to a man they were polite and obviously so anxious to make a good impression that her long pent-up nervousness erupted in an uncontrollable giggle. Soon everyone was laughing as the strange procession moved along the wharf.

As Prudence was handed carefully down the steps to the ground, a small object hurtled from behind a crate and clasped Prudence's legs, nearly upsetting her. Eager hands steadied Prudence, who gasped as she looked down into the upturned face of small, grimy girl-child.

four

"My name's Serena," the child entangled in Prudence's legs said in a rush. "My Uncle Ethan said my mother went to heaven and lives with God, but it's so lonesome here without her. My Uncle Ethan said you were coming to live with us and be my new mother. He said you're a kind lady who will love me and talk to me and read to me. I try to read by myself, but the words are hard to remember. My Uncle Ethan tries to teach me to read the Bible when he's here. But he travels a lot so I don't learn new words very fast."

How grateful Prudence was that Ethan had told her about this darling little girl with copper freckles liberally sprinkled over a tiny turned-up nose, eyes the color of bluebirds and as active. Thick golden braids hung down her back and were tied with blue ribbons whose bows had long since turned into trailing flags as Serena ran.

When Serena paused for breath, Prudence dropped down to eye level and opened her arms to the child. "I'm delighted to be welcomed by such a charming daughter."

"Uncle Ethan said my other mother came to earth to bring me. Then she went back to Heaven." Her little face grew wistful. "I wish she could have stayed a little while with me, though. Uncle Ethan said she went to be with Jesus right after I was born."

Prudence felt tears of empathy sting her eyes and rapidly blinked them into submission. "How old are you, Serena?"

"I be four now, but come the 4th of July I turn five." She drew herself up proudly. "I was born on the same day as

America."

"Well, we'll have to have a great big party to celebrate something so important as your birthday and America's."

Serena's eyes lit like Roman candles. "A real party? With games and cake and presents?"

Prudence nodded and felt her smile widen.

Serena clapped her hands. "I've never had a party. Papa forgets it's my birthday. He works all day on his books."

Yes, little one, Prudence thought, *I can imagine the Fourth of July isn't a happy time for your Papa.*

"Well, this year perhaps we can persuade him to leave the books and join us."

"I knew you'd be wonderful. I prayed to Jesus for you to come, you know." Her cornflower blue eyes, filled with innocent faith, looked so trustingly up at Prudence. "I almost gave up, though. I prayed almost all my life since I can remember."

"That shows a great deal of faith, Serena."

Serena slipped her hand in Prudence's and tugged her to her feet. "But you're finally here. Now I can show you things."

In her excitement Serena rushed along a wide, well-trodden path, pulling at Prudence to hurry. "Under the porch steps is a toad. His name is Solomon. He and I—we're friends. Mrs. Foster hates frogs."

"Who is Mrs. Foster?" Prudence asked, interrupting Serena's nonstop flood of information.

"She's the lady who takes care of me. Other times she cooks for the loggers. She's really nice. But she's awfully busy most of the time. At night she says she's too tired to read to me." Serena crooked a finger for Prudence to bend down. The procession halted while Prudence leaned over. Serena lifted Prudence's hair and whispered in her ear. "It's a secret. I don't think Mrs. Foster can read. But don't say anything. It would make her feel bad if she thought I knew."

Prudence gave the chubby little hand a squeeze. "It's our secret."

Serena nodded and set off again, talking as fast as she walked. "Over there is the lumber office where Papa stays. It hasn't got divides in it. It's one room and he sleeps in it. Our house, Mrs. Foster's and mine, got lots of divides in it. The big bedroom where my papa used to sleep. Well, Mrs. Foster sleeps there now. In another room we have breakfast and supper on holidays when the loggers don't work. It's a big room. It has a fireplace at one end. We sit on the sofa and tell stories and smell food cooking. And upstairs there's two more bedrooms with divides. I sleep in one and you're going to sleep in the other. I moved up so I could be near you.

"I like that we live near the edge of the woods. So many little things live in the woods. I have talks with them when I go exploring."

"You go exploring in the woods?" Prudence asked, thinking that a most dangerous practice.

Serena's saucer eyes widened. "Only along the edges. I can't go farther unless I ask permission."

Prudence nodded and smiled.

The trail turned abruptly out of the trees. There in the clearing was a log house two stories high, and absolutely unadorned. The logs hadn't been stripped, and bark hung in strips from the walls that were weathered to a soft gray. Green moss edged the split shingles and crept into the recesses between the logs. There was a wide covered porch across the front and chairs carved from logs were spotted in conversational groups. One was a large, crude rocking chair with gay floral pillows to soften the unyielding wood. The center door was flanked by two high windows like eyes looking through the forest to the sparkling water of Hartwell Bay.

Standing in the doorway was a woman somewhat over thirty years of age, her white-blonde hair in two neat braids wrapped around her head. She was still firm-fleshed with a trim waist which the sparkling white apron accented. She raised one hand in greeting and the welcoming smile accented her features, generous and symmetrical. Her eyes brimmed with delight, her full voice rang with joy.

"Well, boys, you sure do make a ruckus bringing Miss Beck. You'd think it was the Fourth of July."

The men laughed and their fond looks said they appreciated the woman who cooked their meals. Though several tried to say something, they couldn't compete with Serena's piping voice rising over the rumble. "Mrs. Foster, Aunty Prudence says we can have a real birthday party for me this year. And maybe we can even persuade Papa to come."

A shadow momentarily darkened Mrs. Foster's face, but she managed to cling to the smile. "Why, child that will be special. And I'm sure by July Miss Beck will have convinced your papa a party is the only way to celebrate such an important day as your fifth birthday." She looked with sympathy at Prudence, then came down the steps, extended her hand and pumped Prudence's. "Welcome to Hartwell Landing. There's been precious little work done this morning as the boys waited to greet you." Still clasping Prudence's hand, Hulda Foster shooed the men off. "You've had a good look. Go about your business now, all of you, or Captain Hartwell'll dock you a day's pay." They left good-naturedly, calling for promises from Prudence that she would come to the mess tent for the noon meal so they could see her again.

Prudence allowed herself to glow inside. *But I'm not fool enough to think things are going to be this pleasant when dear Captain Hartwell arrives on the scene.*

While Serena clung to Prudence's left hand, Hulda took the right one and tucked it over her arm. "You're just what this place needs, my dear. Give Jonathan time to chew on Ethan's surprise and get over the shock. He'll soon be putty in your hands." Her eyes swept over Prudence. "Land, look at me chattering on. Come inside the house and let's see about getting you out of those wet clothes. Won't be stylish but I'll rustle up something 'til they get up here with your chests."

She urged Prudence into a steamy kitchen filled the lingering aroma of spiced fruit. "Hope you'll excuse the mess. Been turnin' the last apples of the season into apple butter. Can't do it down at the cook shack. The boys come through soon as they know what I'm about and don't leave enough to fill one jar."

On a large rectanglar pine table stood full Mason jars in rank and file, but Prudence scarcely had a chance to glimpse them before Serena pulled her into another room. "This is the sitting room." She pointed to a doorway leading off it. "Mrs. Foster sleeps in there."

Serena returned Prudence to the kitchen, then dashed to the foot of the stairs where she danced with impatience. "Hurry, Aunty Prudence, Mrs. Foster said I could show you to your room."

"I'm most anxious to see my room and I'm so relieved that I shan't have to stay up there alone." Prudence followed Serena up the steep narrow stairwell to the second floor. At the top were two matching slab doors at opposite ends of a cramped landing.

Serena dashed to the door on the right, threw it open and led the way inside. "This is your room. Mine's across the landing." She pointed a pudgy finger.

Prudence stepped into the most crude room she had ever

seen. Because the sharply pitched roof angled from the center ridgepole to the outer edges of the room, there was nothing flush to place furniture against. And since the slanting ceiling had neither plaster nor paint, the joists and beams and sub-floor showed plainly through the cracks. Only the two triangular-shaped walls at either end of the room were upright, but they, too, were made only of unvarnished raw slabs. Opposite the door and facing west, was a small four-paned window with printed flour sack curtains tied back to a raw wood frame. Now, in mid-morning, little light came through the panes. But from across the tiny landing the sun streamed through Serena's matching window, across the landing and into Prudence's room. The rays fell on the enormous oak rocker next to the tiny window.

Beside the bed and before the low washstand, newly braided rag rugs brought oval splashes of color to the unpainted plank floor. But it was the bed itself that drew Prudence's undivided attention. It was spread with an all-white quilt with scalloped edges and a quilted medallion in the center. Prudence caught her breath when the significance dawned on her. This was called a wedding quilt. She studied the two eager faces before her and wondered if they knew the implication of the spread. "Who chose this lovely quilt to brighten the room?" she asked.

Serena pointed to an elaborately carved chest on the opposite side of the room. "It was in the cedar chest Uncle Ethan brought up from the stored place. Mrs. Foster and me thought it looked pretty."

"It does look splendid and brand new." Prudence laid her reticule on the double bed and the tick rustled under the weight.

"I helped Mrs. Foster stuff your new tick," Serena said, and almost reverently ran her fingers along the expertly stitched pattern of the quilted spread.

Prudence touched the petals of wildflowers in a ragged bouquet in the blue glass jar on the bedside table. "And did you pick the flowers, too?"

A smile wreathed Serena's face. "I went down by the brook. Flowers grow everywhere there."

"They are lovely. Thank you." Prudence bent and placed a kiss on top of the little blonde head.

"And Uncle Ethan found the chest of drawers, too. Everything matches the bed." Serena swept her arm to include the washstand with its delicately flowered pitcher and bowl, a real glass mirror in a gold frame on the wall, the high ornate headboard.

Prudence nodded and smiled as Serena pulled her over to examine the carved golden oak chest with many drawers. "This is my favorite of all," she said. In the sunlight it shone with a deep shimmering glow. Prudence rubbed her hand over the smooth surface and tested the top drawer. It slid out noiselessly and emitted a slight smell of lacquer. The drawer hadn't been used enough to retain the fragrances of the user. It occurred to Prudence that not only the bedspread, but all the furniture was new.

"Isn't this all beautiful?" Serena asked as she patted the rocking chair.

"It is indeed. Where ever did you find such elegant furnishing out here in the wilderness?"

"Uncle Ethan found everything stored way back in a lumber shed. We don't know how the things got there. But he said they weren't doing anyone any good. They should be used. Mrs. Foster polished for hours to make everything shine."

Prudence turned in time to see the color creep into Hulda's glowing face. "Everything is perfect. The two of you have gone to great lengths to make me comfortable."

"Glad to do it. I only. . . ." Hulda quickly clamped her lips tight against the words, leaving the sentence unfinished.

Prudence wanted badly to ask what it was Hulda hoped, but her stolid look said probing deeper at this time would be futile. Hulda took Serena's hand and they watched as Prudence continued her inspection.

The utilitarian black stovepipe that came up from the kitchen stove and continued on through the roof was impossible to disguise. But Prudence didn't mind. Heat radiating from the ugly tube made the room comfortably warm in the damp climate, and she gave thanks. She would at least be warm during her short stay.

"Thank you both for working so hard to make my room so lovely. I feel like royalty with so many elegant things around me."

Unable to contain her joy, Serena danced in circles. "You haven't tried your rocker yet," she said as she took Prudence's hand and pulled her to the large padded chair beside the small window. "Uncle Ethan says he brought this from Seattle before I was born. It's just right for rocking new babies, he says." Serena paused and her large blue eyes fixed on Prudence. "And me," she said softly.

Prudence's stomach knotted. This was the chair he had given Serena's mother to rock Serena in. And then she understood about the furniture, too. This had been the bedroom furniture of Jonathan and Serena's mother. *Oh, dear Heaven, what will Jonathan do when he sees what they have done?* She only hoped she wasn't around when he discovered the furnishings in this room.

"Well, we'd better test this wonderful chair immediately." She unfastened her cloak and Hulda grabbed it.

"I'll take this and while you slip out of your wet skirt, I'll bring you something dry to wear." She disappeared through the door and clattered downstairs.

Prudence did as she was bidden, then sat in the chair. It fit fine. She rocked a little bit and caressed the curved arms of the chair. "Yes, Serena, this chair will rock babies nicely." She held out her arms to the child. Serena climbed quickly into Prudence's lap and curled against her. Prudence wrapped her arms around Serena and began to rock slowly.

"I can feel your heart beating," Serena said in a whisper. Then she reached a tentative hand to explore Prudence's hair and face. "I love you," she said after awhile.

Prudence's heart swelled with her feelings for Serena. "And I love you," she said and placed a warm kiss on her forehead.

"It doesn't take very long to love someone. Does it?" Serena worked her fingers between Prudence's until their hands were braided together.

"No, it doesn't take long at all. Not when you look through the eyes of the heart." And then the only sound in the room was the rhythmical creak of the floor boards under the rockers.

They were both fast asleep when Hulda returned. She hung up the skirt, covered Prudence and Serena with a soft wool lap robe, and crept downstairs to finish her apple butter.

Jonathan stomped into the house carrying Prudence's two larger cases. On the stairs he didn't mind the noise he made, but when he reached the landing he stopped short, then tiptoed through to the door. Silently, he set the luggage inside, never taking his eyes from the sleeping pair in the rocker. Serena was curled in Prudence's lap, their arms and hands woven together until they were one. Her head rested high up on Prudence's shoulder, a look of complete contentment on her little face.

Prudence's head was tipped so that her cheek rested on the top of Serena's head. The weary lines had drained from her strong face and in the filtered sunlight she was beautiful. How was he going to send her away? *You are going to send her away because you aren't going to let this place kill another woman. Losing one wife to this wilderness is one too many. I'll not make it two.*

His gaze left the sleeping pair and studied the room. Why did everything look so familiar? And then recognition rocked him. His face twisted under a fresh wave of grief as he pictured Anna as she lay in that bed. She had not been well during the last six weeks of the pregnancy. She had felt ill and her ankles and hands had swollen badly, her beautiful face pale and puffy. A ball of dread had filled his stomach night and day. He had brought medicine from Seattle, but it had done little good and Anna, her face flushed and feverish, had spent much of each day resting in their new bed.

Finally, early on the morning of the third of July, Anna began her labor. Jonathan remembered how the agonizing hours had dragged by. They had the best Indian midwife in the area, but he had never felt so helpless in his life. Every time Anna screamed, he had flinched and suffered with her. "Is this normal?" he had asked Ethan as the time wore on.

"Yes, Jonathan. There is nothing easy about bringing a new life into the world."

"Then, we won't be having any more children. Not at this price."

Around three in the morning, a seven-pound baby girl was born. Damp tufts of hair the color of spun gold curled over the tops of tiny ears. She was a perfectly formed, healthy child who cried lustily when the Indian woman brought her to him.

He held his daughter while Anna was being cared for. He could still feel that tight little mouth suckling his finger and the tingle of joy that ran through him. Finally, he was allowed to see Anna. He laid the baby in her arms and dropped into the rocker beside the bed, too emotionally spent to say more than, "My dearest Anna, thank God it's over and you're fine."

Anna had gazed at the baby and whispered, "I'm sorry its not a boy."

He stroked her forehead and kissed a spot. "The important thing is that you're all right."

"Isn't she beautiful, Jonathan? She looks just like you."

He had laughed then. "She is beautiful, but it's her mother she looks like."

"I'd like to name her Serena after my great-grandmother," Anna said.

He gently stroked Anna's forehead. "Whatever you want, my darling." He twined strands of her golden hair through his fingers.

For the first two days Anna seemed to recover. She and Jonathan had long talks about their future. Jonathan couldn't remember ever having been so happy. His chest seemed too small to hold his heart. But on the third day her fever flared up again. The Indian woman took the baby from Anna and brought in her sister, who was nursing her first-born.

Though the Indian woman used all her herbs and skill, as the days passed, Anna's condition worsened until she sank into a coma. He and Ethan took turns keeping a vigil at her bedside. Early in the morning on the fourteenth of July, Anna passed from him.

He moved into his office over the mill and buried himself in work. Because Serena looked exactly like her mother, Jonathan could never look on her without feeling the knife of grief pierce his heart.

Who dared uncrate this furniture without first asking my permission? And carted it all up here to be used by this woman who isn't going to be here long enough to dent the feather tick? Jonathan snorted. Of course, there was only one so brazen and sure of himself. Ethan! Several times Jonathan smacked his right fist into the palm of his other hand. Wait until that preacher brother got back here in July. That would give Jonathan time to build a real head of steam. This would undoubtedly be the greatest row they had ever had, and when he was through, he'd bet Ethan wouldn't interfere in anyone's life again.

In the meantime, he would double his efforts to get that woman on a boat, any boat, sailing to anywhere. He wanted her out of here before she upset his routine any worse. She'd already cost him half a day's work. He could ill afford to lose even an hour's work if he were going to keep to his timetable and be financially independent in one more year. Then, he would build a fine house in San Francisco, move there, and maybe. . .just maybe, then would he consider taking another wife. Right now he for sure wasn't going to be stampeded into anything by his well-intentioned but meddlesome brother.

Jonathan looked once more at the sleeping pair. What a peaceful and loving picture they made. He felt his resolve weaken the tiniest bit. Lest he be tempted to let Prudence Beck stay, he straighted his shoulders and firmed his jaw. With fists clenched, he whirled, stalked down the stairs, passed Hulda without a word, and vanished out the door.

five

Prudence vaguely remembered Serena being removed from her arms. In her dreams she struggled to keep the child, but Hulda's gentle voice kept assuring Prudence that Serena would not be taken from her, only undressed and put next to her in the bed. Too weary to fight longer, Prudence was forced to believe the voice and surrender the little girl. She felt weightless as helping hands floated her out of her clothes, into a long flannel gown, lilac scented, and between soft flannel sheets. True to the promise, Serena was placed in the curve of Prudence's body. They adjusted themselves until they fit perfectly. A deep contentment, a feeling of belonging and being desperately needed, flowed through Prudence and she sighed deeply into sleep. However, several times during the night, her body rolled and rocked as though at sea and the motion woke her. Each time she had to adjust to where she was, and each time it became harder to go back to sleep.

Now, in the late hours, with the initial exhaustion healed, Prudence lay in the strange bed and let the awareness of where she was seep slowly into her sleep-befuddled brain. The bed didn't rock in time to lapping waves, but her body still seemed to be in motion. The moon cast shadows of tall pines over the braided rug and plank floor. Serena! Prudence turned to where the child had lain, but the only sign she had been there was the slight impression her small head had left in the feather pillow.

Now, fully awake and hungry, Prudence knew she

53

would never sleep if she didn't find something to eat. Carefully folding back the covers, she stood and the gown she was wearing swept around her. Automatically her hand went to the small bulge below her thickening waist. To any woman with eyes it was abundantly clear that she was pregnant. Hulda knew. Prudence's heart leapt, then sank into the pit of her stomach. Had she told Jonathan? Prudence wished she dared wake Hulda to find out, but in the middle of the night that probably wasn't best.

She tiptoed through the door and out onto the landing. Serena's door was open and Prudence could see the little girl sleeping soundly, a sun-browned arm wrapped tightly around a tattered stuffed dog. Downstairs the moon streamed into the spotless kitchen and the only sound was fluttering little snores coming from Hulda's room.

On the table, covered with a red-and-white checked cloth, a small oil lamp burned low. Its light revealed a plate with a white napkin spread over it and on top of the napkin a piece of paper. Prudence eased her way down the stairs and across to the table.

The note read, "This is the best I could do for your supper since I didn't want to wake you. Hulda. P.S. If you need to talk, I'll listen."

The paper quivered in Prudence's trembling fingers, but she blessed Hulda for having the kindness to keep her findings to herself. And as Prudence blew out the lamp and carried the sandwich up to her room, she felt a sense of relief. At least, now there would be someone with whom she could share her uncertainties, someone who might have answers to some nagging questions about her impending motherhood.

She set the plate on the window sill and folded back the napkin. Her mouth fairly watered at the thought of biting into the fine-grained sourdough bread with smoked salmon between the slices. As she ate, she looked out over the Bay, now calm, with moonlight dancing off the curling edges of the waves. She had been here only a few hours and yet she had never been in a place to which she felt any more attached. Except for a light in one small upstairs window of the warehouse where Jonathan had his living quarters, the big warehouses and the sawmill stood dark and black, silhouettes against the water.

Prudence stared at the light as she ate and pondered. It was full lamplight, not turned low for sleeping. It had to be very late. She found her timepiece on the table next to the bed. It was nearly two o'clock. Jonathan had been up early and worked hard all day. Why would he have his light on at this unholy hour?

She finished her sandwich and poured a glass of water from the pitcher on the washstand. It was two-thirty when she finished and climbed back into bed. His light was still on.

With a sudden startled movement, Prudence woke to the white glare of late morning. She lay listening. The house was quiet and empty. Hulda had probably taken Serena to the cookhouse with her. Quickly, Prudence washed, dressed in a gray cotton dress without the crinoline underskirt and braided her hair into a chignon held in place by a black silk net and plain combs. Throwing a warm knit shawl over her shoulders, she set out to explore her new surroundings. Steam and smoke rose from the shed of the sawmill. The screeching of the saws was eerie and harsh, painfully loud here in the isolated cove. A great mass of logs rode in the water near the mill. All the outbuildings were backed by steep slopes covered with stumps—ghostly reminders of the trees already logged. A carefully laid road of logs led up the mountain in a path of gentle curves and out of sight around a fold of land and heavy brush.

Hartwell Landing looked an orderly, well-run camp, but she would expect no less from anything owned by Jonathan. She was interested in the sights before her, and wanted to know more. Though he had made his feelings about her presence very clear, Prudence was a desperate woman. If it were in her power to convince Jonathan he needed her, she wasn't going to be sent away without a fight. And so, hopefully without appearing to, she looked for him. Giant that he was, it wasn't hard to spot him standing on the timber loading wharf supervising the unloading of the *Thomas Hartwell.*

Prudence positioned herself so that if he chose he could easily see her. He chose not to look up. But by the very act of keeping his eyes glued to the manifest and making it match with the items coming off the ship, she knew he was aware of her presence and making a conscious choice to ignore her.

"That's just fine, Jonathan Hartwell. I have all day and you can't unload that ship forever. You'll have to face me sometime," she said aloud.

The last bit of cargo finally swung onto the wharf. Jonathan gave final instructions for placing the huge stack of items and the reloading of the ship, this cargo of lumber bound for the Orient. He then tucked the manifest in his shirt pocket and walked toward her. As he drew closer she could see the dark circles under his eyes, red from lack of sleep. His face was drawn and there was a tired slump to his shoulders. *Oh, Jonathan, let me stay and help you,* she pleaded silently.

"At least, you had the good sense to stand out of the way," he said, his voice rough with fatigue.

"I worked a good number of years around heavy and dangerous equipment. I know how irritating it is to deal with people who get underfoot." She looked out at the floating logs. "Do you have time to show me about? I find this all fascinating, but I have no idea what I'm seeing."

He frowned and glanced up the sun. "The morning's getting away from me. The figures on this manifest have to be entered into the books, the new items added to the existing inventory, and everything balanced. Plus, I need to go with the crew to see about a problem with the skid road high on the mountain." His shoulders slumped even further.

"I can help with the office work. I've balanced many a manifest and kept a running inventory."

"I can't ask you to do my work."

"You didn't ask. I volunteered. I know this is most presumptuous of me, but you look so weary and seem to carry such a heavy load all by yourself. If you can take a few minutes to show me around, I'll happily work on your books."

He hesitated, eyeing her carefully.

She smiled. "I'm aware you're having to take me at face value, but I can't do a great deal of damage by recording one manifest."

A thin crooked half-smile crossed Jonathan's hard face. He nodded and began to point out various things and offer explanations, making his voice even and matter-of-fact. "That's called a log boom." He pointed to the large pond of logs in the bay at the mouth of the river corralled by a circle of logs cabled together. "We keep the logs in the water because it makes them easier to handle, cleans them for the saws, and makes for less insect damage and rot."

He pointed to the foothills rising sharply above the

water. The slope was covered with stumps of trees, now barely visible inside the dense growth of currant, spirea, thickets of salal and vine maple, young Douglas fir, hemlock, and white fir. "We took some good timber off those slopes, but what's coming out of the deeper woods now is much bigger and straighter. Even when you've seen this western timber over and over again, it's hard to believe the size of the trees. The loggers say it takes three men and a boy standing on each other's shoulders to see up the trunk to the tops of these trees."

As Jonathan talked about the trees and lumbering, Prudence watched as the fatigue fell from his face.

They walked along the wharf and Jonathan carefully handed her down the steps and onto the ground. He went on explaining that the mill produced everything from spars for sailing ships to pilings for wharves and boards and shingles for buildings, depending on the size and type of trees they felled. The lumber went out from Puget Sound not only to the States and Europe, but as far away as the Orient.

They paused where the shay, a little engine with a bell-shaped smokestack, puffed bursts of steam as it waited on the narrow-gauge track for the loggers to finish boarding the open flatcar and take their places on the benches. There was a car behind loaded with chains, saws, and enormous coils of steel cable, a new and very expensive improvement over the old iron cable. "Do you have time to show me where the loggers are working?" Prudence asked.

A surprised but pleased expression enlivened Jonathan's face. "That won't be a problem. The shay makes several trips back and forth." From the ground Jonathan steadied her on the ladder-like steps and eager hands from above saw her safely onto the flatcar. Broad smiles greeted Prudence and she smiled in return.

When Jonathan was seated beside her, the shay began its run past the old cut, up into a magnificient forest, still wet and shimmering from the night. The morning sun, finally high enough to clear the mountains to the east, did its best to dry the moisture. Silvery veils of mist lifted and wove gossamer strands among tall branches. The rank, heavy smell of deep humus rose from the warming ground.

"The forest, like the sea, is an amazing part of our world," Jonathan said as they jolted and swayed along. While they made their way up the mountain, he told how the existence of a forest changed the wind patterns and greatly effected the climate, provided a home for wildlife, determined the composition of the soil, and most importantly for their daily lives, controlled the water supply. "The trees capture the snow, then shade it so it can melt gradually into the thick layer of humus covering the forest floor. All this goes a long way to prevent flooding."

Prudence sensed Jonathan's deep appreciation for God's woodlands and she said as much.

He smiled.

The higher they went, the more dense the brush and the taller the trees until they rode in a world of shadows. Only an occasional lacy filigree of golden light shone through to remind one the sun did exist somewhere above the towering deep-green canopy.

Jonathan stood, waved his hand at the engineer, and the shay belched to a stop. "This is the skid road. If you want to ride the rest of the way to the logging camp, I'll be there shortly."

Prudence concluded that this was much too valuable an opportunity for the two of them to be alone together. She stood and said, "I'd be interested in seeing a skid road, if I won't be in the way."

He hesitated.

"Is the walk to the camp farther than I can hike?"

"No, that's not why I hesitate."

The logging crew was grinning from ear to ear and biting hard on chuckles threatening to erupt.

"There's no real way to explain it. I guess, if you insist, you'll have to experience it for yourself." He reached out a hand to help her to the ground.

Prudence could hardly contain her puzzlement over the men's behavior as she watched the shay chug around a curve and out of sight. The first and overwhelming sensation of the big woods was the absence of sound. It wrapped itself around them, a force of its own. No birds sang, and as they walked along the track beside the road, even the thud and scuff of their feet seemed faint.

"The skids are always at least twelve feet long and each is a foot thick. They are laid exactly seven and a half feet apart. That's so when the shortest log, sixteen feet, is hauled out, it'll always rest on at least two skids and not get caught in between. The runnels or grooves cut into the top of the skids are to help guide the logs. Notice, they're lined with hardwood for longer wear."

As Jonathan talked Prudence studied the half-buried logs laid cross-wise. It was somehow comforting to see the hand of man in this vast wilderness.

And then the sound reached them.

"What on earth is that?" Prudence exclaimed and gripped Jonathan arm, sure they were being attacked by crazed things.

Jonathan's mouth twitched at the corners as he urged her to step to the edge of the trail. "It's the oxen bringing out a load." He could no longer contain the laughter and his shoulders shook with mirth. "I can't wait to see Bull's face when he knows you've heard his performance. You're about to hear the most professional swearing this side of the fiery pit. If it's too much for your sensibilities, cover your ears."

Prudence hadn't long to wait to understand what he meant. The din grew louder. A creaking, clanking, snorting, accompanied by a rumble that vibrated the ground under her feet, all was overlaid by a man's bellowing voice. "Hump along, Red! Move along, Blue! You, Brick, Brass, you get your fat, underworked. . . ."

Prudence's eyes widened at the epithets that grew more colorful as the procession came into view. She clamped her hands over her ears and watched. The oxen were magnificient, eight yoke of them, muscles bulging, straining together in harnesses of wood and leather. Brass caps on the ends of their horns gleamed in stray shafts of sunlight.

The animals dwarfed a slender young man who darted with a bucket of grease in and out behind the last yoke, greasing the skids right in front of the huge log being hauled. But the other man was more than a match for the team. He was a towering block of a man, enormously broad, with muscles as thick as those of the beasts he walked beside and drove. It was his bellowing curses that breached the forest's silence, his sharp prod flicked with the speed of a striking snake, reminding a lagging beast to obey.

He turned from his task and caught sight of Prudence and Jonathan in the shadows. His voice strangled in his throat and his face turned from its usual florid red to beet purple. Before their eyes his head tucked down. He seemed to shrink into himself, the huge body trying to telescope its size.

At the change in their master, the oxen began bawling in alarm and pulling unevenly. The greaser dabbed his own feet and pants with the fish-oiled brush. Bull, rooted to the spot and gawking, fumbled uselessly for his hat and, through it all, Jonathan was laughing so hard he could barely stand. He fought for breath and waved Bull on, saying, "Keep going! We'll see you in camp," before the hysteria engulfed him again.

Bull used the prod like a maestro and got the team moving in step again as he worked up the volume of his running commentary, using substitute phrases for the ones he customarily showered over the backs of his oxen.

Prudence, having removed her hands, joined Jonathan in waves of laughter as Bull would forget, then substitute less violent words into his harangue.

"Almost sounds like he's inviting the beasts to tea," Prudence said, struggling to regain some modicum of composure. "Does he always behave like that when he sees a lady?"

"He's the best bullwacker in the Pacific Northwest, but a lady's man, he's not. He's the only single man in the company who didn't come down to the dock to see you arrive."

As they walked up the shay tracks to the logging camp, Jonathan entertained Prudence with other stories of Bull and his oxen, so that when they arrived they were both flushed and bright-eyed with laughter. Two of the old-time crew members remembered when Jonathan looked like that most of the time.

"Ain't seen him look so light and young since his Anna died," the boss of the camp said to the camp cook, who nodded.

The rest of the men looked up only briefly from their work. Too much time off did them no favor, not when they were paid for the amount of timber they got out of the woods.

The buildings—a cookhouse, a shelter for the oxen and horses, a pigsty and chicken coop, a smokehouse, a small cabin Bull occupied, and a few outhouses—all looked like toys when set against the enormous surrounding forest. Prudence felt that she too had grown smaller, her perceptions confused and altered in this unnatural world. She was at once fearful and enchanted as Jonathan led her into the area where the men were working. Looking up into the tangle of trees overhead, she tripped over a root and Jonathan steadied her as she nearly fell. The caring touch of his hand on her arm made her know how much she could like this man if he would only let her.

"Up this trail, there's a tree that's ready to come down in a few minutes. Want to see it?"

Prudence could only nod as she watched the rest of the crew find safe places to stand as the two fallers moved up a huge spruce, using only their axes and a single board each. They would make a cut higher than their heads, insert the board, and drive their axes deep into the trunk to use as their only support when they pulled themselves up onto the boards.

Like an obedient sleepwalker, she moved when Jonathan propelled her to a safe spot, trusting him to guide her because she could not take her eyes from these two men. They were now opposite the gaping undercut, some twenty feet above the ground.

"They're going to make the backcut now, the last support for the tree." Jonathan's voice was hushed as though speaking in church.

After that, the only sound was the steady rhythm of the faller's axes. Then they stopped. It seemed the forest and all that was in it held their collective breath. The hair on the back of Prudence's neck pricked and she started to scream. Jonathan, watching her, clamped his hand over her mouth before any sound emerged.

The act happened swiftly, but to Prudence time slowed until each second seemed to take a lifetime.

The cry of "Timber!" rang out, then was swallowed by the forest. The tree swayed gently before its voice came, a thin whine, a sharp crack, a groan of pain. At this moment Prudence saw axes spinning thrugh the air and the fallers leaping away and dropping forever, twenty feet stretching into miles.

The sound of the pain increased to an anguished roar as the tree slammed onto the earth, which shuddered with the impact. The air shimmered with floating debris, and an instant of profound silence assaulted the ear drums. The settling noises of the fallen giant broke the stillness, followed by the whoops of the men.

When Jonathan took his hand away, Prudence didn't make a sound. She sagged against him, burying her face against his chest. He thought she had fainted until he felt her trembling against him, heard her trying to talk about the fallers, and understood.

He patted her shoulder gently. "I couldn't let you scream and startle them. The men are fine." He pointed. "See for yourself. I apologize for not warning you what was about to happen. I've seen it so many times, I just didn't think. The only way for them to get clear of the falling tree is to jump. And, just before they do, for safety's sake, they throw their axes. That's a show for their audience. You've inspired the whole crew for the next week."

She pushed away from him and saw for herself that the two men were fine, busily receiving congratulations from the ground crew and looking her way for her reaction. She managed a small wave and a smile. The two fallers saluted her and swept clumsy bows.

Prudence looked at the huge tree and then up at the tear in the canopy of green through which the blue of the sky could be seen. A weak shaft of sunlight sifted down the long tunnel and spotlighted the ugly pillar that only a few seconds before had been a tree growing since the Vikings first set foot on the East coast. The air was filled with the scent of disturbance—a scent of damp earth, ancient dust, and pitch, sharp and new. The pure perfume of death.

She had witnessed death, execution of the innocent, murder. She had heard the victim's scream die in the silence. And she couldn't stop the vision.

Her face was still pale, her mouth trembling, her eyes shining with unshed tears as Jonathan led her back down the trail and seated her on the shay. They rode in silence down the mountain to the landing, and all the way she mourned the destruction of the ancient forest.

She knew she couldn't protect all of it, but if she ever had the opportunity, she would buy and protect as much as she could. It was that promise made to herself and God that returned Prudence to her normal self, much to Jonathan's relief.

six

Prudence and Jonathan left the shay and as they passed by the cook house on their way to the office, Hulda appeared at the door with a pan of dirty water. She flung it off into the woods and waved before she disappeared back inside.

"I'm lucky to have her," Jonathan said. "Her husband is captain of his own lumber schooner. Hulda cooked for my logging crew up on the mountain. They met when he came here for a cargo of lumber. They married and while he sails the seas, Hulda issues supplies to the men from the company store and still keeps the men happy with her delicious meals. Nothing makes men quit faster than bad food."

"You forgot another of her tasks."

Jonathan looked puzzled.

"It is she who, between all her other responsibilities, keeps an eye on your daughter."

Jonathan's face withered and the power faded. "Yes," he said in a whisper. "I tend to forget that task. She performs it with such apparent ease and Serena blossoms under her care."

She doesn't blossom as well as she would have you believe she does, Jonathan. She craves more attention from you and she misses her Uncle Ethan dreadfully. This little angel God sent you needs a family, Jonathan. A real loving family. And she needs it badly.

Jonathan sighed and pulled the manifest from his shirt pocket. "Well, I must excuse myself and begin working on this or I'll never get any sleep tonight."

"You got precious little last night," she said.

His head jerked up and he looked hard at her. "How do you know that?" His voice was gruff with displeasure.

"At two this morning my bed started rolling and rocking like I was still on shipboard. I had no idea one kept reliving the motion of the waves. At any rate, I woke and found I was famished. I prowled the house and found the sandwich Hulda left for me. While I ate I stood in the window. Your light was still on when I turned mine out and went back to bed."

He raked his hair with long fingers and mumbled something about wishing he had an angel to do the office work as he walked toward the warehouse office.

"I'm no angel, but my offer of help is still good."

"I don't take charity, besides, how do I know you can do the work and won't rob me blind?"

How dare he think she would do anything dishonest? *So far you haven't been terribly honest with him, now have you?* Her conscience wasn't going to let her forget she got here by less than honest means. Prudence swallowed the sharp words of defense and said instead, "You can pay me, and you don't know if I can do the work or not. You'll have to take me on faith while I balance your manifest. Taking time out for Serena, I should be able to complete the manifest in about eight hours. Then, if I'm not satisfactory, I'll quit."

"Well, I don't suppose it'll hurt to let you try. Give you something to do until we can get you on a boat and back to civilization."

In spite of their tour and the emotions that ran between them on the mountain, he wasn't going to let her forget, even for a few hours, that her stay was temporary. He turned and moved with long determined strides into the warehouse. Prudence gathered her skirts and hurried to keep up, but her heart was nearly bursting with gratitude. Here was the chance she had been praying for, the chance to be close to him, to work with and for him, the chance for him to see her as the helpmate he so desperately needed.

It was noon and with the saws were silent; their steps on the crude plank stairs echoed through the huge warehouse recently emptied of its store of lumber. After the months of inactivity, Prudence was gasping for breath by the time they reached the landing and entered the small office.

The neatness and organization of the sawmill complex didn't extend up here. Papers and envelopes buried the desk top and spilled onto the floor. Jonathan's bed was a knot of blankets and sheets, his clothes strewed where he dropped them.

His eyes followed her inspection. "Being a man and not given to housework, I guess I've gotten used to this. Hulda gets one of the wives to come a couple of times a month. She does the laundry and cleans the place." He looked a bit flustered.

"I'll bet you haven't gotten used to it at all. But trying to do the work of three or four people doesn't leave a great deal of time or energy for domestic or office tidiness," she said, her voice soft, but business-like. "May I straighten the papers into like piles so you don't have to spend so much time searching for what you need?" She made an inclusive swing of her arm at several manifests flung far and wide in frustration.

"You're a glutton for punishment." He looked over the sorry sight and shrugged his shoulders. "But you're welcome to have a go at it."

"Once we get these records caught up, they won't be the chore they are now." She tipped her head and smiled an angelic smile. "But you have been trying to be all things to all people. Moving your sleeping quarters here into the office so you can work into the night and not disturb anyone gives you no respite from work. You're coming close to working yourself to death, Jonathan. The success or failure of Hartwell Landing is on your shoulders, but broad as they are, they could stand some relief."

Her voice was gentle, and he relished the concern in her face. It had been a long time since anyone but Ethan had looked at him that way.

"Thank you for letting me help a bit." Prudence forced her gaze from him and eased past him toward the large oak desk that filled one wall.

He stood with his feet planted wide apart, hands on hips, his arms akimbo. He didn't know what to say. Everything she had said was true, yet, especially to himself, he kept denying it.

Prudence kept her back to him and fumbled with the litter of papers. She didn't understand fully what was happening to her. Nothing was working the way it should . . .not her heart, not her hands, not her head. She was struck anew with the handsome symmetry of Jonathan's face. The wide, sensual mouth, the nose straight and well-formed, the chin firm and square with that devastatingly deep cleft. But it was his eyes that melted into her soul. They were like prismed crystals. They never stayed the same and in their depths mystery always lurked.

This had to stop. He had much to do and she was keeping him. "If you could take a few minutes and explain how you want the manifest recorded, I'll get to work."

She pulled up the straight-backed chair and sat down.

He walked around the carpet of clothes and brought from the safe by his bed a large black leather-bound ledger. He spread it open across the littered desk and, his voice all business, concisely explained the bookkeeping system.

"Understand?" he concluded, only a muscle flicking in his cheek betrayed any tension.

"Yes, thank you. The system is very little different from what I'm accustomed to."

He eyed her with a sceptical lift to his right eyebrow. "Ask your questions now because I'm going back up to the logging camp and won't be down until dark."

She smoothed the wrinkles from the manifest, and said, "If I should have any problems, I shall make note of them and ask."

He harumphed, something he did, she decided, when he was at a loss for words and clumped rapidly down the stairs.

Before Prudence could settle to her office tasks, she had to bring some order to the chaos surrounding her. She flung open the single window and let into the stuffy room the fragrant air, cool though it was. She whipped off the pillowcases and filled them with dirty bedding and clothes. These she carried down the stairs and over to the cook shack where she deposited them for laundering. Hulda directed Prudence to where the clean bedding was stored at the house. Prudence found Serena playing along the trail and together, they returned to the office with arms loaded.

She heated water on the little jackstove in the corner and, while the bed aired, she scrubbed the unfinished plank floor and made the window and the lamp chimneys shine. She trimmed the wicks and filled the wells with coal oil. Finally, she made the oversized bed and covered it with a colorful tied quilt. And all the while Prudence worked, Serena kept up a ceaseless flow of conversation. She required minimum responses from Prudence. "Really. You don't say. What did you do then? Tell me more," served to keep the tales of adventure rolling from the child until she curled into tight ball atop her father's bed and, covered with Prudence's shawl, she slept.

Satisfied with the physical condition of the room, Prudence turned her attention to the overflowing desk. She made files and brought order to the clutter. In the process she learned about the way Jonathan conducted business and kept the records of it. By mid-afternoon she could begin sorting out and recording the information on the manifest.

Serena spent the afternoon playing outside the warehouse, checking occasionally to be sure Prudence was real and hadn't vanished as figments were wont to do.

When the supper gong sounded, Prudence had the manifest recorded and had begun plowing her way through the backlogged paperwork. On Wednesday the *Thomas Hartwell* sailed for the Orient. It would be at least six months before she returned. The day ended with a bath for Serena and storytime in the rocking chair until she fell asleep in the middle of Hans Christian Andersen's "The Ugly Duckling".

Though Prudence ached with weariness and her baby kicked its protest over the strenuous day, Prudence returned to the office, stoked the fire in the stove, set bath water to heat and laid out clean clothes for Jonathan.

Her steps dragged on the trail back to the house. She prepared for bed, but she couldn't go to sleep until she knew he had returned. It was almost eleven o'clock when the light finally went on in his room.

Thursday, Prudence didn't see Jonathan at all. She worked all day in the office, played with Serena, and again left clean clothes and bath water for him. *If I can keep his personal life pleasant, his paper work organized, his daughter nurtured, he'll change his mind about making me leave. I'm sure of it.* She said this to herself often during

Thursday, Friday, and Saturday.

By supper time on Saturday Prudence had convinced herself that Jonathan had changed his mind. If they could ever see each other and have a few minutes alone, she knew he would tell her as much and her heart sang with anticipation.

Prudence was performing her evening ritual of stoking the fire when she heard footfalls on the stairs. She felt the blood rise in her cheeks and her hand trembled slightly as she placed the last piece of wood in the stove. *This will never do,* she scolded herself. *You're acting like a school girl with her first beau.*

The footsteps stopped at the doorway and Prudence looked up. Jonathan, dust-covered and sweat-stained, filled the opening. "So, I've caught the angel who's been providing me with a warm room and hot bath water each evening. I haven't known such luxury in years."

He smiled, full and warm, and Prudence's heart leaped. There was hope, she just knew there was, and she returned his smile. "You're home a bit earlier than usual and the water isn't quite hot." She set the lid back over the opening. "You look tired."

He pulled the chair from the desk and sat down. "I am tired but tomorrow's Sunday and around here we rest."

"I'm glad to hear that."

"With a minister brother for a partner, do you think it would be otherwise? He had a time convincing me we could accomplish more in six days if we'd shut down for the seventh, but after I tried it both ways, I learned he was right. We used to hold worship service in the cook shack, but now, we gather downstairs in a room built for the sole purpose of worship at the back of this warehouse." He chuckled, stretched his long legs out, crossed his feet at the ankles, and folded his arms across his chest. "What a time we had in those early days."

Prudence could hardly contain her joy. They were actually going to have a personal conversation. With no other chair in the room, she sat primly on the edge of the bed and leaned against the corner of the brass footpost.

"How did you happen to come here?" she asked, prompting him into telling his story.

"My pa and his pa before him were sailors. Fortune smiled on my pa and he finally had his own ship, a fine clipper that sailed the seven seas. When it was time, I went to sea with him, even made enough money to buy some stock in the clipper. Pa was one of the first to anchor at Seattle. He even sailed down the Sound. He liked what he saw, found a buyer for the ship and six years ago, we all came west." His eyes turned dreamy and he rubbed his hand over the square jaw shadowed by the day's beard. "We set up a closed family corporation, with Pa owning 60 percent of the stock and serving as president. He was in charge of the logging operations. I put in my share of the clipper so I owned 30 percent and was the vice-president. Anna, my late wife, donated her dowry. This gave her 10 percent of the stock and she acted as secretary-treasurer of the company. It was she who did all the blasted paper work."

"Another reason you sorely miss her."

A wistful look filled his eyes and his voice was little more than a whisper as he answered, "Yes, another on top of so many."

Quickly Prudence steered the conversation into another vein. "Am I to understand that Ethan has nothing to do with the lumber business?" she asked.

"Ethan, because he chose the ministry, inherited a substantial sum from our paternal grandfather. He was a business man who couldn't walk a beach without becoming uneasy in his stomach. It was his money bought us our first lumber packet." Jonathan chuckled wickedly as he scratched his beard.

Delighted with their growing comradarie, Prudence laughed. "I take it the good gentleman's name was Thomas Hartwell."

"None other." Jonathan rubbed his face with the palms of his hands. "Nothing itchier than a beard this old."

"Are you planning to grow it out?"

"No. That bed looked too inviting these last few nights. I haven't taken the time to shave. I'll get it off in the morning."

"If I may be so bold, I'm an excellent barber and could soon rid you of the beard and the itch which will surely make your sleep uneasy."

He looked skeptical.

"My references are impeccable," she said as she stood and moved toward the shelf where the shaving mug and razor were. "When my grandfather lived in our home one of my duties was to shave him daily. Soon my father entrusted his beard to my hands." Prudence set the shaving materials on the desk and spread a sheet over Jonathan. As she stropped the razor's edge, she said, "As I caught up your books, I was impressed with the way you've managed the company. Though you started woefully undercapitalized and have drawn only a small salary, you will soon begin to reap considerable returns." After testing the sharpness with her thumb, she set the razor aside and poured hot water from the teakettle into a dented metal basin and brought it to the desk and dropped in a towel.

Jonathan glowed under her praise. "The profits have been used to purchase equipment, enlarge the mill, buy timberland and logging rights. I ordered the latest improvements to upgrade the sawmill. The new machinery should be in San Francisco by the time the *Anna Hartwell* gets there with a load of top-grade lumber. I've put every spare cent into this new equipment." A shadow crossed his face. "I wish I was there to see to the loading. The crates must be placed in such a way that they are kept dry and rigid all the way here. I would have captained the ship myself, but I was the only one who could negotiate the lumber contracts in Seattle.

"If our luck holds and that ship makes it home from San Francisco safely, we'll have the finest sawmill on the Sound. We can fill those contracts I signed in Seattle and we'll have the first money surplus since we started."

Their conversation came to an end as Prudence wrung out the towel and wrapped it around Jonathan's face to soften the whiskers. As she worked, his head gradually rested back against her and she prayed the baby wouldn't decide now was exercise time. Only a few kicks and all was quiet. When Prudence was finished, Jonathan slept soundly.

Prudence's heart twisted at the sight of the exhausted man asleep though he sat upright in the chair. She poured his bathwater and laid out fresh clothes before she shook his shoulder gently to rouse him. Slowly, he opened one bloodshot eye and took in the surroundings before opening the other.

"You're bath is ready, your clothes are laid out, and your bed is turned back. I'll leave now and see you in church in the morning."

Jonathan stood and the sheet she had covered him with slid to the floor. With the white bunched around him hiding his feet, he looked like he was standing on a cloud. "Before you go, we must have an understanding," he began. "You have worked miracles in the short time you've been here. Serena is a different child, you have

added civilized comforts to my life, my office is function-
al, and everyone speaks kindly of you. But no matter how
wonderful you are, and you are an exceptional woman, I
am not ready to take a wife. This wilderness killed my
step-mother, it killed my Anna. It will not take another I
love. I made that vow on Anna's grave and I reaffirm it
many times each year.

"As you well know, I am not financially able to leave.
With the rebuilding of the east after the War, the demand
for lumber is strong, but any disaster—a depression, the
mill burning, a lumber-filled ship wrecked—anything
would wipe me out. Until I can see a solid future here and
be able to run my holdings from a base in Seattle or San
Francisco, I will not consider taking a wife."

It was as though he had read her mind, had been reading
it for most of a week. Prudence hoped to hide her humiliation but her face dropped and she knew he could see the
tremble of her chin as she fought the tears.

"Your company is pleasant," he continued, his voice
softer, more gentle for he knew he had hurt her badly. "At
another time and in another place perhaps we could have
made a good marriage." His voice strengthen and his jaw
jutted forward. "However, you're not going to stay so we
can find out. You will still leave as soon as the *Anna
Hartwell* returns from San Francisco and we get her
loaded."

seven

Having accompanied Prudence to the house, Jonathan found himself reluctant to leave the fragrant warmth of the cheerful kitchen. He stood with his hand on the doorlatch and studied the room as though seeing it for the first time. Though it galled him to do so, he had to admit Prudence had a real knack for making a house a home. Even in the few days she had been in Hartwell Landing, she had added such touches as new curtains to the kitchen windows, stitched while she waited nightly for Jonathan to turn off the light in his office-bedroom. Bright yellow daisies on a white background made the room seem filled with sunshine on the darkest, rainy day. And he hadn't heard a word of complaint from her, even when he knew she must be aching with weariness as she was now. He knew this because as she finished icing the cake for Sunday dinner, she bit the corner of her lip and then some time later she knotted her fist and rubbed the middle of her back.

"You going to bed soon?" he found himself asking.

Her head, bent to inspect the side of the four layer cake, popped up and her eyes, those great green eyes, widened perceptively. "A rather personal question, don't you think, Mr. Hartwell?" Her eyes twinkled and she tilted her head to match her teasing smile.

Jonathan clamped his jaw shut. For him to make such a suggestive remark, the woman must have addled his senses worse than he'd thought. He'd better get out of here fast before he said something else, something he would really regret and look like a fool taking back. "Church is

77

at eleven in the room at the back of the mill. Please plan to attend and bring that wild child of mine."

Handing the frosting-covered knife to Serena to lick, Prudence said, "Serena and I will be so proper, you may not even recognize us." Laughter bubbled under her words, and Serena giggled and squirmed with delight.

Jonathan stepped out onto the porch and shut the door on her teasing words. She seemed completely unaware of how beautiful she was and when she relaxed and lowered her guard, she was even more desirable. As he walked by moonlight toward his austere living quarters, he wondered if that were the reason he seemed to go out of his way to bring such expressions to her face.

Prudence had given little thought to beauty. She had learned at the tender age of three that she wasn't even pretty. "A sad mistake of nature" was the way her beautiful younger sisters phrased it. Her mother never contradicted them, and mirrors gradually became enemies to be avoided. Prudence glanced in mirrors mainly to see if the plain twist of hair she wore low on her neck had caught all the strands.

But after the way Jonathan kept looking at her in the kitchen today, she had to know, really know if she were pretty enough to attract a man. Not one who married her out of pity the way Frederick had, but one who truly wanted her. One who thought of her in his dreams, waking and sleeping. One who thought he would die if he couldn't have her with him always.

This morning when she dressed for church, she pulled the pins from her hair and let the thick, rich brown strands tumble. She shook it free over her shoulders and arranged it to frame her face. In the gold-framed mirror next to the washstand, she looked at herself with different eyes, blocking out the cruel words of her sisters. "Plain as toast."

"A face that stopped clocks, that's why we can't tell time at our house." She studied her face like it was a map of some unknown country.

She didn't wonder if she were pretty enough. That was vain, and she had finally learned after much heartache that mirrors didn't tell everything. She knew change was coming and wondered if she would be equal to it. She wondered and searched the eyes of the woman in the looking glass, but she was no more learned than Prudence.

Prudence and Serena were in their places on the front row bench. Nearly everyone in the community was present. After the opening hymn, accompanied by Hulda playing the asthmatic organ with little skill, Jonathan came forward and conducted the service.

He made an imposing figure as he stood behind the elaborately carved cedar pulpit. His dark brown wool shirt and cream cravat blended with his tiger-striped hair and deep tan. He stood erect and poised, a natural leader, with the air of one in complete command.

The devotionals reminded Prudence of Tyngsboro and home. Every Sabbath for as long as she could remember, all the Becks gathered at the same church and shared the front rows. The number of front row seats needed increased yearly until now the family occupied the first four rows. Either her father or one of her uncles lead the service and had since Prudence could remember. She never thought it would be so, but today she missed her family, even her spoiled sisters.

During the long months of the voyage she had thought about Jonathan and dreamed many beginnings to a new life with him. During the days she worked in his office, she had clung to the hope that he would change his mind and let her stay. But on Friday night when he had made his feelings sun-bright clear, only a complete fool would think he would change his mind. *And though I would be hard pressed to prove it, I am not a* complete *fool,* she told herself.

She drew a trembling sigh and, because no matter how hard she tried, she could not yet face thinking about her future, Prudence forced herself to concentrate on Jonathan's message. He was reading from the fourth chapter of Philippians, "...whatsoever things are honest, whatsoever things are pure, whatsoever things are lovely, whatsoever things are of good report; if there be any virtue, and if there be any praise, think on these things." He fixed her with a stern eye while he carefully placed the large, black leather Bible back on the pulpit.

Jonathan, still pinning her with his eyes, said, "When one practices deceit, even a small deceit, regardless of the reason, that person is an abomination in the eye of God and man. Without honesty, nothing that person does or says can be believed. And though the person repents of the sin, it requires time for the sincerity of the repentance to be accepted by the injured parties."

A heavy, breathless silence filled the room and Prudence looked to see if the eyes of the congregation had joined Jonathan's in his scrutiny of her. At her glance, their eyes drifted back to Jonathan and he shifted his gaze.

She had repented of her dishonest letter, repeated those vows many times over. However, she would do it again if it kept her baby safe from a life of prejudice. Maybe the Lord wasn't happy with her repentance. When you repented you weren't supposed to be willing to commit the sinful act again. Given the same circumstances, she was afraid she would make the same choice.

Prudence bowed her head and bit her lip. She stared hard at the cracks in the rough floor and forced herself not to blink out the tears that flooded her eyes.

Serena slipped her hand inside Prudence's and she looked over into the upturned little face, confusion clouding the sky-blue eyes. "Is it something my papa said that makes you cry? I don't understand." She crawled up into Prudence's lap and rested her head under Prudence's chin.

Prudence didn't understand either. Was he trying to talk himself out of his feelings for her? And he did have feelings for her, despite his valiant attempts not to let them show.

Prudence cradled Serena close and let her thoughts drift to her own happy childhood days, blocking out Jonathan's stern lecture.

After the service, the congregation, and it was of a goodly size, formed a welcoming circle around Prudence. Serena tucked herself into the folds of Prudence's skirt and clung tightly. Jonathan approached, stood at Prudence's elbow and introduced her to each family, love for his workers filling his fine, deep voice.

She was surprised to see how young they were—all younger than she, she was certain. Nearly all carried babies, and those that didn't soon would be. Most of the women wore drab gray linsey-woolsey dresses and brightly-colored hand-crocheted shawls over their heads to protect their hair from the ever-present wind. The men, most of whom looked considerably older than their wives, had on red plaid lumberjackets and wool trousers tucked into their "corks"—logging boots with sharp spikes that shredded the surface of any plank floor.

Prudence felt the warmth and honesty of these people. She liked them all and longed to become a permanent part of the community of Hartwell Landing.

The reception over, Prudence wanted to talk to Jonathan about his sermon, but not with Serena present. Or maybe she should leave well enough alone.

They walked outside into the beautiful day, a rare day with the sun shining in a cloudless sky. When they returned to the house, Serena turned her most innocent face up at her father and said, "Can we go on a picnic?" She cocked her head and eyed Jonathan.

"It won't take a minute to prepare the food," Prudence said and even as she spoke, she laid her hat and shawl aside and slipped into her big apron.

"I don't think that's such a good idea," Jonathan said to Serena. "I have alot of work to do."

Prudence looked up from the cold roast she was slicing. "This is the Sabbath, Jonathan. You told me you honored the Sabbath here and it is one of the Commandments, the fourth to be exact. No work except that of an emergency nature is to be done."

He blushed to his hair roots and opened his mouth to retort, but Serena slid into the pause. "Oh, please, Papa. We can take the Indian canoe. You can paddle us up the river. I'll take you to my favorite place."

"Do I know where it is?" Jonathan asked her.

"I don't think so."

"If we have to take a boat to get there, that sounds like a mighty long way from home. Much too far for a four-year-old to be roaming." His smile disappeared and his face returned to its usual stern set.

Serena gulped and slid her hand inside his. "Almost five," she corrected. "Besides, Mrs. Foster knows where it is and I always tell her when I'm going there."

Jonathan looked at Prudence, but she lowered her eyes. This was the first time she had heard Jonathan behaving like a parent, and she had no intention of interfering.

"Papa?" Serena's voice was scarcely a whisper and her eyes flooded with pleading.

Without warning Jonathan laughed, a wonderful deep rumble and his whole countenance lit. What an irresistibly handsome man he was when he smiled. "How can I fight two such bewitching women?" He reached out and tousled Serena curls as she squealed and hugged his knees.

Within an hour, they were on their way in the cedar dugout canoe gaily painted with Indian symbols. As Prudence trailed her hand in the water, she felt happier than she had in months. For the first time since her arrival, Jonathan seemed to release his responsibilities. She watched him now, his rugged face red with exertion as he fought the current. His eyes were on Serena and his expression filled with contentment.

He shifted his gaze toward the trees along the shore and asked, "Did you know that anyone can file a claim for a hundred and sixty acres of timberland?"

Had he read her mind? Excitement rose in Prudence. "What does such a claim cost?"

"A small fee and after certain provisions are met, the land's yours. That's how my family started the business. We all filed for our acreage. Of course we claimed the frontage around the Bay. That way the company controls what goes on up here. That timber's all been claimed, but it would be helpful if this area right here were tied up." He pointed toward a towering grove of old trees some distance upstream from Hartwell Landing.

Imagine being able to own timberland of my very own! This was an opportunity that would pay for her baby and give them both a solid future until she could get on her feet. Her senses reeled. "But I thought I couldn't stay. How can I file a claim if I'm not here?"

"The land agent is coming Tuesday or Wednesday on a routine inspection."

"What if I'm able to claim that hundred and sixty acres

and you want to log it? Even though I won't be here, will you pay me for the timber that's cut?"

He looked at her with disgust. "Certainly, the going market rate at the time of harvest. Once this virgin timber is cut, the second growth will come, and we'll have to pay you again to cut that."

Prudence's eyes shone with the prospect of getting paid twice for the same claim. She might never have to worry about money again.

"Of course, it takes years for the trees to replenish themselves and grow large enough to be logged. But the cycle does go on and on."

"Oh," she said softly. "In other words, if a person owned enough timberland, he'd be set for his life and beyond."

Jonathan's eyes narrowed ever so slightly and he looked hard at her. "That's right. Assuming, of course, that the stand is located close enough to a mill to make logging it practical."

As if you have any money to make any purchase beyond the original claim, Prudence dear.

A rise in the land made small rapids in the river, and rowing became more difficult. Jonathan had no more breath for talking. Prudence concentrated on the passing forest while her thoughts whirled until Serena broke the silence. "There, Papa." She pointed and Jonathan swung the canoe out of the current and beached it on a sandy stretch.

Jonathan gripped Prudence's elbow to help her out, and once again his touch sent a warm rush through her.

"We have to walk some," Serena said. "Follow me." Importantly, she set off into the forest along an animal trail.

"I had no idea Serena wandered this far away from home," Prudence said, as she picked up the blanket.

"Nor did I. I'm not pleased that she has this much freedom. I think I need to set some clearer boundaries." Serena disappeared around a bend in the trail. "Wait for us," her father called, carrying the wicker picnic basket. "I hope this special place isn't too far. I'm starved after all that rowing."

"It's not," Serena assured him as she came back down the trail.

Happily, Prudence followed Jonathan through the woods, walking over the soft, rich earth, delighting in the mix of fragrances from the ancient trees and the damp soil. Through the fir and cedar boughs that arched overhead, the sun's rays cast a golden, slanting path. With each step Prudence's sense of awe and reverence grew more and more intense. This untouched wilderness, growing since the time of Christ, was a holy place. She looked at Jonathan's broad back and wondered if he felt the spirit of the woods.

"We're here," Serena announced.

They stepped into a grassy meadow dotted with wildflowers. A babbling brook meandered through the center and all around the edge of the clearing were rose-purple rhododendrons with their thick evergreen leaves and pink azaleas clustered in full bloom. A black-tailed deer, grazing at the far side of the meadow, looked up, sniffed until she caught their scent, then with one bound disappeared into the dense underbrush.

They found a flat boulder at the edge of the brook and Jonathan spread the blanket over it. Prudence set out a packet of sandwiches and cookies and a jar of lemonade. Serena took her sandwich and went off to explore.

As Prudence ate, she sighed with contentment. "This is paradise."

Jonathan smiled and looked around. "I agree. Right

here, on the south side of the river is one of the finest stands of timber found anywhere. I suspect it's the exposure to sunlight and the air currents and a steady supply of rain."

"Does your company own it?" she asked.

"No. It's public land, under the jurisdiction of the Land Office. Most of the Hartwell holdings are on the north side of the river. We have a great deal of excellent forest, but none so fine as this."

"Why didn't you claim this land as well?"

"Don't think we didn't want to. But when we came to this country six years ago, it took all our claims to secure the beach property. We've been lucky so far that this stand has gone unnoticed and unclaimed."

Prudence replaced the leftovers in the basket and Jonathan shook the blanket. Then, he spread it on the ground, stretched out and was soon sleeping deeply.

She sat on the rock that had served as their table and studied the surroundings woods. It beckoned to her, beseeched her to take it, keep it safe from the saws and axes. And she heard its voice. It would take her last penny, but she would file that claim when the land agent came. That way she could protect a tiny corner of the old forest.

She wondered how Jonathan would react when he learned of her action. Would he rage until he turned purple? Or would he understand why she wanted this particular section of trees. He could cut some of them, but she would choose which ones. He should certainly be willing to agree to that.

eight

It was Tuesday when the small sidewheeler that carried the mail entered Hartwell Bay and announced its arrival with a shrill blast from its whistle. Word spread like a runaway forest fire through the camp. Sea gulls squawked and swirled overhead as if they, too, understood the importance of the arrival of the mail. Women left their cabins, small children in tow, and hurried along the dusty paths to the wharf. The millhands turned off the big saws and gathered with their families.

Barnabas joined Jonathan at the place where the boat would tie up and unload. Jonathan stood with one foot planted on a coil of thick rope and tried hard to concentrate on the boat doggedly making its way toward the dock. However, Prudence kept infiltrating his thoughts. He could still feel her gentle touch as she shaved him last Saturday. In fact, he had to fight not to spend his time reliving every moment of their evening together and Sunday's picnic.

Now as she approached, he wondered, ever so briefly, if he were really going to be able to send her away. He had never known such a capable and striking woman. This morning her soft brown hair waved around her face and the large loose coil at the base of her neck was held by a rose-colored silk net. Her flawless peach-colored skin glowed with health. He tried hard not to look into her wide green eyes framed by long curling lashes, but they drew him like a magnet. It was only with the greatest determination that he forced his gaze to return to the mail boat instead of watching Prudence as she mounted the stairs and walked briskly toward him.

Prudence look at Jonathan with guarded eyes. All of Monday she had fought the insidious need to see him and won. But today, the more she busied herself the more she felt the compulsive craving to be with him. Hearing the whistle blast of the mail boat gave her the perfect opportunity without looking as though she sought him out. The pain at having to leave was growing more intense after each encounter with him. She could not allow herself to do more than see him.

The sidewheeler cut through the water and nudged against the wharf. A deckhand tossed a line to Jonathan, who tied it to a pile. While they exchanged pleasantries the captain heaved the mailbag onto the dock and handed the packages into eager hands. Barnabas handed over the outgoing mail sack. When it was safely on board, Jonathan loosened the line, threw it onto the deck, and the boat pulled away and into the channel.

Jonathan carried the mail sack to the end of the pier, opened it and began handing the letters into the hands of the crowd of eager young men and women.

"Prudence," Jonathan called, "here's a letter for you." He noted before he handed it to her that the postmark was Tyngsboro, Massachusetts. She had never told him where she came from or anything about her family. This handwriting was fine and feminine. Her mother, perhaps? "Oh, yes, and here's a package, too. Unusually heavy for the size of it."

"Thank you," she said politely, her reserve indicating she would not welcome more conversation.

Well, what did you expect she'd do when you keep

telling her in no uncertain terms that she isn't wanted here? That you're sending her away on the first available boat to anywhere.

Prudence took the letter and small box wrapped in plain brown paper. It was heavy. She walked to the end of the wharf where she could read her letter in private. The handwriting was her mother's and the return address did not include her father's name. Slowly, carefully, she eased free both sides of the flap down to the sealing wax. Then, breaking the seal, she took out the heavy ivory vellum. Her fingers trembled as she unfolded the paper and read:

> *My dear daughter,*
>
> *I take pen in hand to tell you that your father passed from this mortal plain on April 1st. He was riding a spirited young stallion, not well-trained. It threw him and he landed head-first in a ditch. We are all well. Your sisters came to be with me for two weeks. I am alone now and beginning to reorder my life. I shall remain here in Tyngsboro, though both girls tried endlessly to entice me to come live with them. This is the first time in my life I am free to be myself. I went from my parents home to my marriage bed and have been   d i c - tated to all my life. With you and your spirit of independence as my courage, I want to see if I am capable of running my affairs. I know I find   the thought of trying stimulating.*
>
> *My first independent act is to send you the package which I hope you have received at the same time as this letter. I can only hope the contents are not too late to help you. Please*

write and tell me know all about your adven-
ture.

Your loving mother,
Evangeline Beck

Prudence felt little sorrow over the death of her father. He had expected her to be the son he so desperately wanted. It made his disappointment even greater when she looked so much like his family.

Prudence put the letter in her pocket and retrieved the package. The paper was stout and Prudence worked to get at the box inside. There was another note inside the box. "Your father always showed favoritism toward your sisters. Now it's your turn. This is your dowry. It's enough to give you a bit of security. Use it for something you want. All I ask is that you spend it wisely, my dear."

Prudence gave a little cry as she searched through the cotton to find several small round objects, each wrapped in tissue paper. She chose one and unwrapped it. It was a hundred-dollar gold piece. Quickly, she wrapped it back up and returned it to its place.

Prudence reread the letter until she had it memorized, then she slipped it back inside its envelope. Clutching the box to her chest, she made her way down the wharf and, her eyes swimming with tears she refused to shed, found her way to the house and her room. Only when she was safely behind the closed door did she allow the tears to fall. Tears for all the verbal abuse and humiliation she suffered at her father's hand until she could escape. Tears for the years her beleaguered mother had endured the poverty her tyrannical husband imposed on her. Tears for the courage it took for her mother to keep what was rightly hers. To face down two spoiled, dictatorial daughters for whom all the gold in all the national banks wouldn't be enough.

After the tears, Prudence washed her face and set out her fortune across the bed—thirty gold pieces, three thousand dollars, and she knew exactly what she would spend it on. But where to keep the money? The box was too obvious. She needed an everyday container that would be overlooked as too common to hold something precious. She sat in the rocker letting her gaze roam the room until she came to the tobacco can that held her hairpins. *Perfect!* Lining the bottom of the can with some of the cotton, she layered in the gold coins, all thirty of them, and covered them with more cotton. On top of that she replaced the hairpins.

The next day Prudence, in what had become part of her routine, was at work in the office, trying to contain her anticipation and keep her mind on the books when the room darkened. She looked up from her writing to find that Jonathan had stopped by. He filled the doorway but came no closer. "Word has it that the Federal land agent will be here sometime today," he shouted over the whine of the saw blades.

Prudence's pulse quickened at the thought of the agent coming so soon and she dropped her pen.

A puzzled looked shadowed Jonathan's face as he watched the pen roll to the floor. "You all right?"

She felt a blush rise as she nodded and retrieved the errant pen.

"Though the office is the last place he'll check, keep your eye out for him. If he doesn't come before noon, I won't see him. I'll be up at the logging camp, but I'll be back around four. Keep him entertained until then."

"Is there anything he needs to know that I can show or tell him?"

"No, his visit's just routine. He comes around every so

often on an inspection tour to make sure we're not logging over public lands. We're dangerously close in one section and I want his approval on the last few trees that are ours."

Jonathan disappeared, but Prudence didn't go back to work. She sat thinking about the wonderful forest where they had picnicked on Sunday and the claim she intended to file.

Prudence was on her way back from the house with the necessary two dollars and fifty cents for filing fee when the land agent pulled his launch up to the wharf. She waited for him at the door to the warehouse.

He was a middle-aged man with a dark beard sprinkled with gray, wearing a tweed cap perched on a thatch of bushy gray hair, and carrying a roll of maps under his arm like most men carried a shotgun. He shifted the roll from his right arm to his left, doffed his cap and said, "I'm Sam Wilson. So you're the new lady." He squinted through gold wire-rimmed spectacles, looking her over thoroughly. "Heard you was a right pretty addition to the Washington Territory. After seein' for myself, I'd say they was ungenerous in their praise, if you don't mind my saying so."

Prudence didn't mind in the least and smiled widely. "Pleased to make your acquaintance, Mr. Wilson. I'm Prudence Beck."

"Ran into Preacher Ethan and he said you come out to marry that old grouch, Jonathan Hartwell, and he won't have none of you. He's the smartest man on the Sound when it comes to business, but in every other way he's about the dumbest."

Prudence couldn't agree more, but that a complete stranger should know so much about her situation caused her some discomfort. Were she and Jonathan the talk of the whole Sound? She chose to ignore the agent's comments and said, "Jonathan is up at the logging camp and will be back about four. Have you eaten?"

"Such as it was, about eleven. Wouldn't mind a piece of Hulda's pie, though."

"And I'm sure she'd love to serve it up. She just finished whipping the cream for strawberry pie and making a fresh pot of coffee."

"Now that's a welcome a man won't soon forget."

"When you finish, I'd like to do some business with you."

His right eyebrow rose. "Now, that makes me curious enough to do the business and then have the pie."

"One should never allow business to come before fresh strawberry pie, Mr. Wilson. What I want to discuss can wait at least that long."

He looked torn, but the pie won.

When Sam Wilson returned, he was almost purring with contentment. "That woman makes the best pie on the whole Sound. Makes me come around more often than I have to, the thought of her pie does. But here I prattle on when you and I have business. What is it you're interested in?" He plopped his roll of plot maps on top of the desk, untied them and pulled one from the stack. "I'm chancin' you're looking to make a claim."

Prudence nodded and drew up chairs for them both.

He rolled out the map and anchored the corners with paperweights. "You'll see here on the map where the Hartwell holdings are. I've traced around them in red."

For a long time Prudence studied the plot map. She could see the outline of Hartwell Bay and the river twisting its way to the Sound. She made mental notes of which was Hartwell timberland and where the adjacent unclaimed plots lay. It thrilled her to think of owning land—something that made her a part of this wonderful country today and would bring her a bit of income in the future.

She followed the line of the river to the spot where they had spent Sunday afternoon. There it was, her forest, unclaimed. Those fine trees on the south side of the river, plus river frontage to someday float the logs to the Sound would be hers and her child's. The money from the lumber would be security for them and she could pick the trees they could cut. She wouldn't allow it to be clear-cut like Jonathan did his land, leaving it nothing but ugly, rotting stumps. She would have a beautiful forest for the rest of her life.

She pointed to the map and asked, "Would it be possible to make my timber claim along here?"

Mr. Wilson hesitated. "Since you don't have a logging operation to get out the lumber, are you sure you don't want your claim to border Hartwell property?"

Prudence feigned innocence. "Is there a reason I shouldn't consider this river frontage? I was there the other day with Jonathan and Serena, and it was so peaceful. Almost like a sanctuary."

"That's a prime stand, right enough." Mr. Wilson drawled the words. "Just one problem I'm looking at. When they first come to this country Jonathan asked me to save that particular claim for him." He scratched his bearded chin and stretched his neck growing red as a spawning salmon. "He wants to buy it soon as he gets some spare cash."

"*Buy* it! You mean you have public land for sale?"

"Why, yes, ma'am."

The excitement nearly choked her. "How much is it?" she asked in a pinched voice.

"Prices are down a bit. We're only getting two dollars and fifty cents an acre."

Her jaw dropped and she stared at him in astonishment. She had no idea timberland was so inexpensive. With her dowry money she could buy twelve hundred acres of the finest forest in Washington Territory. And because it could be cut over at least once more in her lifetime, it would give her security for years to come. She sent a silent thanks to her mother and knew she would approve of this purchase. Nothing could provide more security than choice acres of prime timber.

Having made up her mind, she said, "I'll file for my hundred and sixty acres, and then I'll buy twelve hundred acres. I want this section here on the south side of the river."

Mr. Wilson gasped. "But ma'am, that'll cost you three thousand dollars!"

Prudence smiled. "I'm well aware of the cost, Mr. Wilson. I have the money. Give me five minutes and I'll be back with it."

Prudence pushed her chair back.

Mr. Wilson turned a worried face to her. "I...I...well I promised Jonathan...."

"Mr. Wilson, I know for a fact that it will be some time yet before Mr. Hartwell can buy that land. If I buy it and give him all rights to the lumber, wouldn't that be the same as his owning it?"

"Well, I do feel I owe Jonathan the right to let him tell me it's all right with him if you buy it. I think I'll wait on my answer until I see him this afternoon."

Prudence chewed the corner of her mouth and pondered this unexpected reversal. "Mr. Wilson, do me one favor. I'd like to be a part of the discussion with Jonathan about this purchase. Will you please bring him here to the office after the two of you have concluded your business?"

The taut lines left Sam Wilson's face and it returned to a more natural color. "I'll be right glad to make that arrangement. Won't mention what you got up yer pretty sleeve. Let you be the one to spring it on him."

Prudence smiled and saw Sam down the stairs. Though she tried to keep her mind on the books, she found herself daydreaming of her empire as though everything was already settled. Even then, the afternoon dragged until it seemed an eternity before she heard hobnail boots on the stairs.

The two men pulled up chairs and Sam once again spread out his maps. He let Prudence explain her plan.

"Jonathan, you have taken me into your confidence and entrusted me with all the financial records." She waved her hand over the still-open books, her handwriting filling the pages. "Barring any sort of misfortune, at best it will be at least a year before you have enough money to make this purchase." She turned to Sam. "There are other logging companies seeking to purchase fine timber, are there not?"

Wilson nodded.

"Now, because you can't legally refuse to sell to someone with the ready cash, how do you think Mr. Hartwell would feel if some competitor forced you to sell that stand of prime timber to him? At least, if I buy it, it would always be available to the Hartwell Lumber Company."

She turned and looked at Jonathan. His face was outlined against the rays of afternoon sun, the strength of every feature like a stone carving. His jaw was set, his mouth grim as he stared at the map as if mesmerized by it. *What had she done to the man who had become the center of her world?* She saw a muscle move in his hard, sculpted cheek. Didn't he understand that she wanted this for him, for them? Her voice trembled as she asked, "Do you have an objection to such an arrangement?"

Jonathan appeared lost in thought and while he was, Prudence hoped he couldn't hear the pounding of her heart. She had wanted only one other thing this much in her life, to marry Jonathan Hartwell, and since that wasn't to be, this would at least serve as a tie between them. Perhaps it would be the force that made him change his mind one day.

She added some more to her argument. "We would have a binding contract. The timber would be available only to the Hartwell Lumber Company. You would have exclusive rights to cut it and it would safe from the hands of a competitor. That's all you want, isn't it?"

Jonathan nodded without looking at her. "I guess that's the reason for owning any timber, all right."

Sam Wilson pulled a large red bandanna from his back pocket and wiped his forehead.

"Then, Jonathan, please let me buy it for the Hartwell Lumber Company."

Sam Wilson didn't tell them that every lumber operation along his part of the Sound was cash poor right now and he hadn't made a decent sale this quarter. It would look real good on his report if he could make a sale of this size. And as this very bright lady pointed out, what difference if she owned it or Jonathan owned it? She had ready money and it might be years before Jonathan would have that kind of spare cash.

Jonathan nodded his agreement, but he looked like he was agreeing to his own execution.

"Oh, thank you, Jonathan." Her face turned radiant and

she clasped her hands as though to keep from clapping her joy.

Sam wasn't going to delve into the reasons for Jonathan's moroseness. "You fetch your money, Miss Beck, while I start on the papers." Her delighted smile sent even Sam Wilson's old heart tripping. If he were home more, he'd try his hand at courting this lovely lady. How could Jonathan Hartwell be so blind?

In no time, Prudence was back with her cache of coins. She had thought to remove the hairpins before leaving her room, but now she pulled out the cotton and spread the coins on the desk. From her apron pocket she produced the necessary amount to pay the filing fee on her claim.

Finally, Mr. Wilson finished his paper work, counted the money, and said, "Sign right here." He pointed to the line at the bottom of the page. She dipped the pen in the inkwell and wrote her name in a strong firm hand.

"Well, my dear, it's all yours, three thousand one hundred and sixty acres of the best timberland in the Territory."

Prudence held the deed to her land with visibly trembling fingers as Mr. Wilson packed up his roll of maps. He fished the large railroad watch from his vest pocket and consulted it. "It's after four. Word of a sale like this'll spread fast. Don't want to be totin' money of this kind after dark." He rattled the coins inside the tanned leather bag and tucked the map roll under his arm. "It's been a pleasure doing business with you both." He wanted to tell Jonathan to come about and stop being so stubborn before he lost this extraordinary lady. But for once in his life, Sam Wilson just shook hands with Jonathan and kept his mouth shut.

Prudence got up and followed the agent to the doorway.

Jonathan was right behind her.

"Now, little lady, don't you be standin' on manners. I seen myself outta this place for years. Reckon I can find my boat without an escort." He tipped his hat and started down the stairs.

"You can probably find the boat without an escort, but I doubt you can carry all that money without some help," Jonathan said, but the attempt at humor was forced.

When they were gone, Prudence held the deed to her heart and let out a great whoop. The sound was absorbed by the constant whine of the saws, but she knew she had done it and it felt so good, she whooped again. Then, sedately she sat down at the desk, propped the deed against the coal oil lamp where she could glance at it frequently as she worked. She worked steadily until the saws shut down and she realized it was six o'clock. Where was Jonathan? Surely he didn't go back up on the mountain. Little nagging concerns worried around the fringes of her mind as she gathered the big black ledgers and stored them in the safe. While she was cleaning her ink pens, she heard the bronchial hoot from the little engine on the narrow gauge railroad. It came bringing the loggers home from their day's work in the woods. A half-mile from camp the engineer always blew the whistle so the women in camp would know their hungry husbands were near. Hulda would be rushing around in the cook shack putting finishing touches on supper for the majority of workers, single men who ate at long oilcloth covered tables and slept publicly in rows of beds in the bunkhouses.

The door at the bottom of the stairs opened and someone bounded up the steps, two at a time. Jonathan burst through the doorway and walked straight to the desk. "Where are the books?" he growled.

"They're in the safe where they're normally kept. Is there something you wanted to especially see or discuss?" She started toward the squat, little safe Jonathan used as a bedside table.

"Nothing that can't wait until morning, I guess."

"Didn't things go well on the mountain?" She reached for her shawl and wrapped in around her shoulders.

"Just about as usual. One of the trees fell wrong. . . ." His hand shot out and snatched up the deed she had left propped against the lamp. "Yes, there is something I want to discuss," he roared and loomed over her, waving the deed in her face.

She took a step backward and clutched at the shawl. "What are you doing with the deed to my land?"

He read the deed carefully, then appeared to read it again. "Twelve hundred acres you bought! You bought my timber. You've been telling me how poor you were. That you didn't have enough money for your fare to San Francisco. When did you come into this kind of money?" His eyes widened and the red that mottled his throat spread into his face. "What was it in that package you got yesterday?"

"Not that it's any of your business, but it was my inheritance. My mother sent it to me with the instructions to buy something special that I wanted."

Between clenched teeth, he said, "And you had to have that particular plot." He began pacing the floor, his spikes gouging splinters from the planks with each step. "You bought the south side—*my* land!" He slammed his right fist into the palm of his left hand.

Prudence stood, stunned, mute as a totem.

Jonathan stormed up to her, looking about ten feet tall as he towered above her. He waved the deed under her nose. "You knew I had spoken for that plot. I told you and I know Sam told you." His eyes sparked and he leaned over until their noses nearly touched. "And in spite of that, you bought my ground!"

"Jonathan! You said it was all right for me to buy it. If you felt this way, why did you agree to the purchase?"

"You left me no choice. You have a right to buy land, any land that's available. You know I have no money and you broadcast that fact to all of Puget Sound."

"I only told Mr. Wilson," she said in a small voice.

"That's like sending a telegram, only faster." He slammed the deed down on the desk. "You know what I think?" He stabbed the air with his forefinger in the direction of the river. "With all the thousands of acres for sale out there, you just had to have my land!"

She straightened her shoulders and glared back at him.

"I think you bought it just for spite. To get even with me for not marrying you."

Now it was Prudence who tossed out angry words. "That had nothing to do with my selection of timber to purchase. You told me what good lumber those trees would make. Besides, now you don't have to worry about some competitor coming in and staking claim to those wonderful trees. You may cut my trees as long as they're the ones I give you permission to cut, and pay me a fair price. That's all you want the land for, isn't it? For the lumber?"

For the blink of an eye, an unmistakeable sadness shadowed Jonathan's features. Then he straightened and loomed over her. He still wasn't through. "You claimed your hundred and sixty acres, didn't you?"

She nodded.

"And where, pray tell, are those acres?" His voice dripped with sarcasm.

Prudence answered quietly. "Those acres stretch along the south side of the river and border the other land. We have a long, skinny stretch to give us lots of frontage. That will make harvesting the trees much easier, won't it?" she asked. *What was the matter with this man? She had done all of this for the good of them both, and he was acting like an injured party.*

He threw the deed onto the desk so hard it skittered across the surface and came to rest against the lamp, and then he stomped toward the door. "If I weren't completely convinced before that you were the wrong woman for me, I am now. From now on, I shall thank God daily that I stood firm against our marriage."

"And I, sir, shall also thank Him for the same blessing." Prudence couldn't believe she was speaking such nonsense. Her tongue seemed to have taken on a will of its own, completely bypassing her brain.

Her words were lost on Jonathan, however, for he stalked out, slamming the door behind him.

nine

Jonathan stood at the end of the wharf and looked anxiously at the thick fog bank moving slowly across the bay from the northwest. This meant the Juan de Fuca Strait and Puget Sound would be fogged in. Coming through Admiralty Strait between the peninsula and Whitby Island was a tricky stretch of water where numerous currents converged and, if conditions were right, created a turbulent, heaving sea. To make matters worse, there were sharp rocks that could slit a hull and sink the ship like a rock. The *Anna Hartwell* was loaded to maximum weight, responding sluggishly at best, and a heavy fog was the last thing the crew needed to safely navigate this difficult stretch of the trip.

He prayed they had secured all the guy lines that lashed the crates of heavy machinery. He shoved his hands deep into his yellow slicker pockets and clenched and unclenched them. He would give almost anything right now to be there to double check every inch of those lines. If those cases weren't kept steady and allowed to slide back and forth on a tilting deck, the precision of the new equipment would be distorted. After all this expense the wood products coming from the mill would be no better than they were now.

The cold mist descended, blotting everything from sight. Jonathan stood, his shoulders hunched, stared into the gray wall before him and tried to ignore the feeling of foreboding that swept over him. He could stand inactivity no longer and stalked off the wharf and along the trail toward the silent mill.

The fog was so thick he nearly collided with Prudence before he could see her. He exploded, needing to rage at someone, to unload some of his apprehension, and she was an easy target after what she had done to him. "What're you doing out here at this hour?" he roared.

She jumped backward a step, pulled herself straight and set her jaw. "I didn't realize one had to have your permission to walk the trails of Hartwell Landing," she snapped back at him.

"Don't you get smart with me, Miss Beck! Life here was steady and predictable until you waltzed in and stirred everything into a fine stew."

Suddenly, her defiant gaze melted and her features softened. "It's the ship you're worried about, isn't it? Isn't the fog like it was when we came down from Seattle, here for only a few hours?"

Jonathan raked long fingers through his tousled hair. "It's possible. Or it could hang around, thick like this, for a week."

Her lips pursed into "Oh," and that's all she said.

He pushed past her and started up the trail. She swung around and walked with him. *Makes herself so much at home she doesn't even ask permission to come along*, he fumed.

"What would you do if you were captaining the ship?" she asked, breathless from keeping the pace he set.

He stopped and turned. "I'd sail north to Vancouver Island and anchor at Cook's Bay until it was clear." He looked into fog, now so thick he couldn't see the wharf from where they stood. "But I'm not captaining the ship, and the man who is has a family here and he's been gone a long time. He'll be anxious to get home to his pretty little wife and those three lively boys."

"And you're worried he'll chance the fog's clearing soon and try the Strait."

Jonathan nodded and thought again of the letter he'd received when the mail packet last came. His captain, Benjamin Mason, wrote that the lumber had been sold for far more than they had expected. That meant there would be sacks of gold coins locked in the safe in the captain's quarters. The new equipment he was bringing for the mill would increase production and give a wider variety of building materials. When the ship docked, he would have enough to pay the men and keep things going until the next load could be sold. That load would bring profit, real profit he could use to buy more land. He gave Prudence a sour look. He had been so close to owning that prime piece she bought from under him.

Another thought crossed his mind. Maybe she would sell it to him at a profit. After all, she wasn't going to do more with it than let him log it. He liked thinking about that, but he'd wait until she was ready to leave before he sprang the idea on her. The money would look more enticing if she were going away with only meager funds.

Right now though, he wanted to think about the *Anna Hartwell* and her cargo. It made him nearly sick to think his whole future lay in someone else's hands. Not that Benjamin Mason wasn't a fine captain and as capable a sailor as rode any sea. But Jonathan never completely trusted anyone. How he wished he were the one sailing his ship. He could feel the wheel in his hands, hear the waves slapping against the hull, see a dolphin leap and dive alongside, taste the tang of saltwater spray on his lips, smell danger in the thick shroud of approaching fog.

Helpless, Jonathan could only pray Mason was headed for a safe harbor until this fog lifted.

Since the workday had been extended an hour to cut as much timber as daylight would allow, Jonathan had been eating his night meal with the men at the cook shack instead of sharing supper with Serena and Prudence. This morning when Jonathan went over the books with Prudence before he boarded the train for the logging area, he had complained that the long hours on the mountain this week had kept him from spending much time with Serena. Prudence wondered if it were the work that caused him not to come or his anger at her. She still couldn't believe she had said she wouldn't marry him. How could she have lost such complete control? Those hot words had undone all she had so carefully worked to establish between them. She would have to begin all over and now there was so little time.

When Prudence finished the small amount of book work, she left Jonathan a note. Serena missed him sorely, Prudence said, as she knew he missed Serena. She suggested that he have dinner at the house tonight. Serena would nap and be up so he could play with her and read her a story.

Now as the mantle clock chimed six, Prudence gave the kettle of beans a final stir and moved the fresh beets to the back of the stove.

Serena's little button of a nose was pressed against the front window, straining to see through the fog that still lay in a heavy blanket over land and sea. For once she was quiet so they could hear the engine whistle's special signal, three short blasts.

Prudence looked around with satisfaction. A fire crackled pleasantly in the fireplace at the end of the large kitchen. The table, spread with a freshly laundered cloth, was set with three places. A charming bouquet of red roses, Serena's contribution, served as the centerpiece, their fragrance mingling with those of the cooking beans and freshly baked bread.

"He's here! Papa's here!" Serena shrieked as she rushed to pull open the heavy door. Jonathan hadn't even washed the dust from his face. A face that grew more drawn each day the fog remained. He had read the note and come directly up to the house. He still wore his corks and they gouged into the wooden floor of the porch, leaving a trail of splinters as he walked to the door.

Prudence winced. She would have to sweep again so the slivers wouldn't catch in the hem of her skirt and prick her ankles. But having Jonathan here was worth any inconvenience. It would give her another opportunity to work at making him understand why she had chosen that particular piece of land to buy. And maybe, just maybe, he might soften his stand on making her leave. *Prudence, dear optimistic Prudence. You need your heart examined.* She firmed her jaw. She would continue to pray for these miracles, even though she had no reason to think anything had changed between her and Jonathan.

"Papa! Papa!" Serena whirled into her daddy's legs and clung as they played their little game. She stood on his foot and grasped one leg. He walked the length of the room, all the while trying gently to shake off this "thing" that had attached itself to him.

"Prudence, something is gripped tight to my leg. Have you any idea what it is?"

"Perhaps it's a lost raccoon from the forest."

"It's me, Papa. It's me, Aunty Prudence." Serena squealed and laughed uproariously.

"Why, so it is. Do you have a hug for me?" her father

said, his voice filled with laughter.

He picked her up and she threw her arms around his neck in a great hug. Then, gently she patted his shoulder and rubbed her cheek against the rough checkered jacket he still wore.

"Oh, Jonathan," Prudence said in a whisper. "Serena is so precious and she adores you so completely."

A quick look of pain crossed his face and his great hand splayed over Serena's back as he pulled her tightly to him. "I'll admit I haven't been the father I should have been, but that's going to change. I intend to move back into this house and occupy the room which is, for the moment, yours."

Serena pulled back and looked from Jonathan to Prudence and back again. "If you sleep in that room, where will Aunty Prudence sleep? Will she sleep with you like Mrs. Foster's husband does when he comes home from sailing?"

"Aunty Prudence is leaving on the *Anna Hartwell* as soon as she arrives and we get another load of lumber aboard."

There was a long heavy silence in the room. Serena turned a stricken face to her father and her chin trembled with unshed tears. Silently, she pushed herself from his arms and fled up the stairs.

Jonathan colored slightly and poked at the fire in the fireplace. Prudence fussed with the table settings to hide her heartbreak. Her question about leaving had certainly been answered. Jonathan left no doubt and no room to negotiate. Still, Serena's feelings should be considered for once.

"Jonathan, I know there's no hope for us, but what would it hurt for me to stay, do your office work, and make a home for Serena?" She paused, looked up at him from under her eyebrows and thought, *And for you, if you'd let me.* Instead, she continued, "Serena's so lonesome and we do get along splendidly."

Jonathan stormed the length of the room until he stood before Prudence. With his forefinger, he raised her chin until her eyes were locked into his deep brown ones. Quickly, she looked down at the checkered pattern of the tablecloth.

"Miss Beck, look at me and listen. Really listen to what I am saying, because I mean every word and there is nothing. . .I repeat, *nothing* on the face of this earth that will make me change my mind."

He leaned closer, and she felt the warmth of his breath on her face. It smelled of peppermint and she found herself wondering if he had plucked a sprig along the path and nibbled it on his way to the house.

He snapped his fingers in front of her face and she blinked. "Prudence Beck, stop denying we're having this conversation. Now listen closely to what I am about to say, and believe it. Believe every word. How dare you use my child to win my acceptance. You have made me realize my neglect and I accept my failure. That can and will be changed. On the other hand, you lied to me regarding everything about yourself, and that cannot be undone." He felt anger build with every word. "You are not trustworthy. You are not honorable. You are not welcome. You are not going to stay. The *Anna Hartwell* should be here in the morning. I want you ready to go on board. You will stay on the ship while we load. In that way, I'll be certain of your whereabouts until we sail."

"You're going to captain her?" she whispered.

"I certainly am. I want to personally deliver you onto

a schooner bound for Boston."

He swung about on his heel and walked out onto the porch, closing the door behind him. His corks ground into the wood of the porch as he stomped across it and down the steps.

Prudence dropped into a chair. She stared at the door and listened to the hiss of the lantern and the crackle of the fire, the only sounds in the room. The vein in her neck pulsed. The top of her head tightened like the skin had shrunk. Prudence ran a hand down the front of her unfitted apron. The baby kicked hard and constantly like he was showing his sympathies were all with Jonathan. Then, slowly she eased herself onto her feet and climbed the stairs. Serena was curled on her bed, asleep, smeared tear tracks highly visible on the tanned cheeks. Little hiccups still interrupted her breathing, and Prudence felt her chest tighten until her heart had no room to beat. With her own tears streaming down her face, she wrapped Serena's arms around her favorite stuffed puppy and closed the door.

Once inside her bedroom, she pulled out the valises and set them on her bed. Systematically, she packed, leaving out only the necessary toilet articles for morning and her black traveling suit.

Prudence turned out the lantern and, as she did each evening, looked out her window toward the upstairs window that was Jonathan's room in the warehouse. Tonight, like last night, only a wall of swirling gray met her gaze. She felt separated, cut off from him, and a crippling desolation swept over her. How could she go away and leave Jonathan and Serena? How could, survive if she left her heart here?

Morning dawned clear. The Bay sparkled with dancing sunlight and the damp from the fog burned off. With

Serena bathed, fed, read to, and cuddled before she skipped away to play, Prudence was free to do the washing.

After she hung the laundry on the line, she stood back to watch the wind with each fresh gust change the choreography of the clothes. Such a simple thing and yet it renewed her soul, made her know this was the place she belonged, made her know if she left she would not survive and neither would Serena. A sharp chill traced its way along Prudence's spine, and she shivered despite the warm rays of the late May sun.

Suddenly restless, Prudence walked briskly down the trail toward the mill and out onto the wharf. She breathed deeply of the pitch-scented air and thrilled at the magnificence of snow-covered Mount Rainier in the distance. She had no idea how long she stood there, but when she turned away sails were visible as a schooner entered the mouth of Hartwell Bay.

Her heart paused in the regularity of its beat and Prudence felt her body stiffen, become wooden. The *Anna Hartwell* was home. She supposed she should spread the news of the ship's arrival, but her devastation was such that she could only lean against the wharf railing and watch. But as the boat drew closer, she sensed something amiss. The hull sat too high in the water for a ship as loaded as Jonathan's ship was said to be. And then the name, *Tanner,* became clear.

What in the world was the *Tanner* doing down here? Her regular run was from San Francisco to Seattle and back. Surely, Jonathan wasn't so angry he had sent for Amos Sperry to come to take her away.

As the ship approached, Barnabas joined Prudence at the end of the pier. His normally expressive face was a blank. Only his eyes showed his apprehension. "Toss me the line," he called to the deckhand, and quickly the *Tanner* was snubbed tight.

Captain Sperry's beard-covered face appeared over the railing. He tipped his cap and called, "Morning to you, Miss Beck. Ye look like ye've settled in right well. Got some roses back in those pale cheeks, and that apron says ye be about womanly things."

Prudence looked down at the full apron. Yes, it still covered her advancing pregnancy. "Nice to see you again, Captain Sperry. What brings you down our way?" she called.

"I have need to see Jonathan Hartwell. Is he here?"

Prudence had seen nothing of Jonathan since their embattled parting last night, and she looked at Barnabas.

"He's expecting the *Anna Hartwell* sometime today and he's in the sawmill getting things ready for the new equipment," Barnabas said. "I'll go get him, if you'd like."

"I'd like," Amos Sperry said and set his lips in a grim line that said he would prefer no more conversation.

In the silence while they waited for Jonathan, foreboding surged through Prudence. Whatever Captain Sperry had to say was bad news, she was sure, and she shoved her hands deep into her apron pockets, picking nervously at the inside seams.

Jonathan did not appear, and the waiting wore on Prudence. Finally, she could stand the inactivity no longer. "I can't imagine what's keeping Jonathan. I think I'll go along and see if Barnabas has missed finding him somehow." As she walked into the cedar grove, she glanced back at the captain. He was standing on the deck of the *Tanner*, a long parcel tucked under his arm. Now she broke into a run. "Jonathan!" she called, and hysteria shrilled her normally low, melodic voice.

"Right here," he answered as he rounded a turn in the trail. "What's the matter? Is it Serena?" he asked as she whirled around and started back down the trail.

"No." She told him about the arrival of the *Tanner*. Unaware of the act, she grabbed Jonathan's arm impulsively. "Though Captain Sperry hasn't said as much, I'm convinced he bears unhappy news."

Jonathan picked up the pace and Prudence, unable to keep up, gathered her skirts and trotted behind him.

"This is a surprise, seeing you down this far in the Sound, Amos," Jonathan said as he stepped onto the plank and boarded the ship. The two men shook hands and Captain Sperry helped Prudence onto the deck.

"This is a visit I'm taking no pleasure in. I think you both better sit down." He motioned them to a bench against the bulkhead. Then, he laid down the parcel he held and began. "It's fearful I am that I bear sad tidings, but I thought you ought to know. We trailed the *Anna Hartwell* along the coast. She was loaded and sat deep in the sea, so we kept her in sight all the way. . .just in case. When we came to the Strait, the fog dropped over us with no warning. Gave us no choice but to sail north and anchor in Cook's Bay until it lifted. Couldn't see from bow to stern, and we sat idle for three days. When it cleared last night, we pulled anchor and put into Seattle at daybreak. Didn't see no sight of your schooner along the way, though. Just had to come down and see for myself that she got in safe." He looked slowly around the bay. "She hasn't come in, has she?"

The color drained from Jonathan's face. "It's been foggy here for the past three days, so we haven't been expecting her until today."

"I hope they didn't try going through the Admiralty Strait in that murk. Probably waited it out in some other cove. Only thing that gives me pause is some fresh wreckage strewn along the rocks off Hood's reef."

A soft moan escaped from Jonathan.

Quickly, Prudence said, "Could they have had cargo for Seattle and gone there to unload it?"

"They didn't have room for anything extra." Jonathan's voice was barely a whisper.

"Could have been transporting some gold and important papers. I wouldn't give upon the idea of them being a messenger. Though I unloaded me ship before I came down here and they hadn't been there then. Could have come in after I left, easy enough."

Jonathan, his face ashen, tried to smile. "I suspect you're right, Amos. You know Benjamin. Tries to pick up extra dollars to buy timberland every chance he gets."

Captain Sperry reached for his canvas-wrapped bundle. "When we saw the wreckage on the reef, we anchored at a safe distance in the Strait and some of the hands lowered a boat and rowed to the reef. They brought back the largest piece they could carry." He motioned to a knot of sailors standing at a respectful distance, and two of them approached carrying a large parcel. They unwrapped the canvas to reveal part of a mast. The broken ends were freshly splintered, obviously from a recent wreck.

Jonathan knelt and ran his hand over the wood. "I don't recognize it."

Captain Sperry's face relaxed and he smiled. "Glad to hear it's not yours. Sorry about getting ye all riled for nothing, Jonathan." He bent and threw the tarpaulin over the broken mast, and his gaze lingered on the shattered wood. "Always hate to see a ship go down like that. Means they spent considerable time being battered before they finally sank." He motioned for the sailors to take the wreckage off the ship. "It was worth the trip to see you again, Miss Beck. I'd try to persuade ye away from this life, but we're heading north to Alaska. That's no country for a woman. Not even hospitable for a man." He smiled wanly as he looked at Jonathan's still pale face.

Placing a possessive hand lightly on Jonathan's arm, Prudence reached and shook the captain's hand. "Thank you for the offer, but I love Hartwell Landing and am quite content to stay here."

Jonathan cast her a sharp look, but said nothing beyond thanking Captain Sperry for sailing out of his way to tell him.

After the *Tanner* turned and sailed back up the Sound, Jonathan knelt beside the bulk on the wharf, threw back the canvas, and slowly ran his hand over the broken piece of wood. "I'm sure this isn't from the *Anna Hartwell,* but on the off-chance, however slight, I'm going to take Barnabas and the fishing lugger. It's fast and maneuverable. We can stop at the lumber ports between here and Seattle. I'm sure we'll find the schooner safe."

Prudence stared at the broken mast and felt the warm May sun turn chill.

ten

The waiting was worst of all. Prudence scrubbed the entire kitchen floor on her hands and knees. Then she ironed the clothes, washed every window in the house, and when she ran out of housework, helped Serena float little boats along the river to the Bay. They picnicked in the early evening, setting out their supper under Serena's favorite tree at the edge of the forest near the house. Afterward they rocked in the big old rocker on the porch while Prudence read stories to the little girl until she fell asleep.

When Prudence lay down on the bed, hoping to sleep the night away in oblivion, a rush of worry about Jonathan swept over her, and she got up again to pace. Finally, she dressed and went through the star-filled night down to the warehouse and his room. There, she lit a lamp. She touched the things on his desk, stroking the pen he most often used, handling it as if she thought it might shatter with the touching.

She studied the books on the shelf above his bed, studied them carefully, looking for the most worn volumes, his favorites that would give her clues into the facets of his personality. She smiled when she found one on horticulture. What on earth did he plan to grow? Gently she lifted it down and turned to the marked chapter. Tree farming. She skimmed the pages that told about clear cutting and replanting the entire area with seedling trees which would grow to ideal harvestable size in thirty to forty years. She must talk with him about this new idea when he returned.

She replaced that book and took down the one beside it, a thin volume on pure mathematics, its pages as worn as the horticulture book. *What an intriguing man. He dislikes the tedium of keeping the accounts, but enjoys the mental challenge of complex mathematical theories.*

The next book was the biggest shock of all. As worn as the other two, it was Mrs. Browning's slim volume of poems, *Sonnets from the Portuguese.* That this would be one of his favorites seemed completely out of character. Her hand trembled as she read the inscription. "Dearest Anna—I cannot begin to count the ways. You hold my heart always, Jonathan."

Prudence felt her own heart alter its rhythm as despair settled in. She could fight for Jonathan's love against a flesh and blood woman. But against an angel, she held no weapons. Prudence returned the book to its place and, the strength gone from her legs, sat on the bed. On the safe beside the bed lay Jonathan's Bible. He must have forgotten to take it. She picked up the dog-eared volume and ran her fingers over the scarred cover, the warmth from her hand releasing the faint smell of worn leather.

There was a bulky marker midway in the book, a photograph, overexposed and blurred, but still much too clear. Anna. Neither the overly busy painted background or the stiff pose beside a horsehair chair took anything away from her beauty. Her dress buttoned to the high collar, but the fit showed beautifully shaped shoulders and the swell of firm breasts, and the crinoline-supported skirt billowed from a tiny waist. Her hair was piled high on her head in an elaborate style, away from the slender neck, framing her exquisite face.

Prudence's knees buckled and she sagged into Jonathan's chair. The small, perfectly carved nose over the teasing

mouth and eyes which shone brightly despite the flat limits
of the picture revealed Anna's beauty. But it was the
tremendous sense of joy, the exuberance for living flowing
from her that made Anna irresistible. She must have been
looking at Jonathan instead of the photographer. Even the
amateurish composition of the photograph couldn't hide
the laughter and promise, teasing and tenderness that
spilled from Anna. And it was all for Jonathan. All her love
showed so that a stranger would have to be blind not to see
what had been, what still was between them.

The portrait was probably used as a marker for his daily
Scripture reading, placed where he saw it at least once
every day, perhaps even more often. For all its vitality, it
was only a shadow of the real woman. It served only as a
symbol, for his remembrance of Anna was undimmed and
had remained intact in his heart for the four years she had
been gone.

With this knowledge Prudence felt old, old and shriv-
eled in body and soul, an ancient crone who had been born
ugly and would never in her life look nor act even remotely
like Anna. At last, she realized what it was that Jonathan
had been trying to tell her. Anna was the kind of woman
a man never forgot. Her light was so intense that after
nearly five years, it continued to burn undiminished in the
heart of her mate. For Jonathan, Anna wasn't dead. She
was just away on a trip and would return one day. Prudence
understood now that he would have regarded himself an
unfaithful husband were he even to consider courting
someone else, and a bigamist if he remarried.

With great care, she returned the picture to the Bible, put
the book back in its place, and forced herself to think how
she was going to get through the next days until Jonathan
returned with the *Anna Hartwell*.

She trudged with heavy steps up the hill to the house. When she finally slept, her slumber was disturbed by the restless flutterings of half-realized nightmares, and she was glad when the morning light awakened her, glad the weather still held against a storm which would make the search for the *Anna Hartwell* difficult and prolong Jonathan's absence. Understanding how futile any effort was to win his affection, she decided that when he returned, she would offer him her land at the price she had paid. Knowing how strapped he was for money right now, she would ask only for the first payment, enough to keep herself and her baby until he could get the new machinery set up and operating. After he was more solvent, he could pay off the balance.

The first day Jonathan was gone stretched into a second and then a third.

Though Prudence was not a good sailor, she was the descendent of seafaring men and not unaware of the danger. No matter how brave or how skilled the sailor, he was constantly at the mercy of the sea. Often during these lonely days of waiting for Jonathan's return, she thought of the seaman's prayer, "Protect me, O Lord, because Thy sea is so vast and my vessel is so small."

She was also haunted by Jonathan's remarks that the ship would have to sail past an unlighted reef. He had not had to spell out the danger the reef presented in a storm or heavy fog and how there should be a lighthouse to warn the ships in the Admiralty Strait. Prudence tried to convince herself that Benjamin Mason had taken the schooner into Seattle to deliver some papers or gold brought there for extra profit. The ship would be coming into the Bay any time now.

Several times a day she made excuses to pass the

sawmill and ask Barnabas if there had been a sighting of any ship. "You're fretting yourself sick, Miss Beck. You'll see the schooner come sailing in here right soon, and Jonathan right behind." But the longer they waited for news, the more distraught they all became.

Finally the fishing boat came home alone. The minute she saw Jonathan's face, she knew the news was bad. A numbness settled over her as she waited with the millhands who had gathered on the wharf. Their faces mirrored her own despair.

Barnabas met Jonathan as he stepped onto the dock. Struggling to control himself, Jonathan said, "The shipwreck was the *Anna Hartwell*. All hands and all cargo were lost."

Prudence still clung to a slim hope. "How can you be sure?"

One of the crew in the fishing boat handed a piece of wood to Jonathan, and he held it up so they could all see the letters TWELL painted on it. "We searched the shore for wreckage. This piece of the bow from the *Anna Hartwell* was lodged in some rocks. We figure the schooner hit the outer tip of the reef and ripped such a hole in the hull that it sank before anyone could abandon ship. It's nearly two hundred fathoms deep right there." His voice broke. Prudence understood what that meant. He had lost everything, including his finest ship. But not even Jonathan knew how little he had left because she kept the books that told the grim story, while he drove himself and the men to fulfill the orders that would make them all rich.

At the enormity of the loss, financial and human, Prudence staggered and sagged against the railing. Barnabas wrapped a strong arm around her and kept her from falling to the decking. Jonathan moved quickly to her side. "Any of the crew on the lugger can answer your questions. I'm taking Miss Beck up to the house. Barnabas, close the mill for the day and send word up to the loggers. We'll hold a memorial service at ten tomorrow morning."

With Jonathan's support, Prudence made it back to the house. He saw her upstairs and seated her in the rocker. "Thank you, Jonathan. Why don't you try to get some rest? You look exhausted."

He gazed at her, his eyes glazed with pain. "I must go down to see the families of the men lost."

"I don't think you should right now. You need some time alone to regain your composure, else you'll bring no comfort to those families. I'll fix dinner. It will be time enough for visiting after you've rested and had something to eat." She rose from the chair and stood facing him.

He made no further argument. She threw the quilt back and helped pull off his boots. He stretched out across the wide bed and she tiptoed down downstairs.

The next morning, the adults assembled in the cedar grove for the memorial service. Barnabas got through the eulogies and the prayers and, when he couldn't go on, Prudence read from the Psalms. Then, to the surprise of all, she began singing "Rock of Ages" in a clear, sweet voice and everyone joined in.

Jonathan took the floor. "I'm going to take advantage of this time while we're all assembled to tell you frankly where we stand so you can make plans." The energy, the power that brought and held people to him was gone, leaving only flat words listlessly spoken. The congregation stirred like restless children.

"It's still months before we can expect the *Thomas Hartwell* and the profit she brings back from the Orient. I was counting on the sale of the lumber to square accounts with all of you, with bonuses besides. Of course, every-thing went down with the *Anna Hartwell*. What little cash I kept here I will give to the wives of those we lost. They can return to their families. For the rest of you, the best I can do is issue scrip which can be used for necessities at the company store or redeemed later for cash when we sell more lumber."

"What about insurance, Jonathan? Didn't you carry any on such a valuable vessel and cargo?" one of the loggers asked.

"I did, indeed, but settling the claims will take months, which means we can't purchase a new schooner immedi-ately. As many of you have commented, there are more and more vessels from all over the world making their way down the Sound looking for good buys on lumber. For the next while, the best I can see for us is to sell from the wharf." As he talked, his confidence returned and his voice resounded with promise. "If we make our prices compet-itive, the word will spread quickly, and I'm convinced we'll get buyers for all the lumber we can mill."

He paused and let his gaze sweep over the despondent group. "Those who are willing to stay under these circum-stances will get a bonus with every sale." He smiled wanly. "That will continue until we're operating normally again. Those who'd rather leave and go to another camp have my blessings and goodwill. We heard in Seattle that there is a new camp up and running across the Sound to the west of us. I'm sure they're looking for good men and I can testify that you're the best."

His voice cracked and he paused again to regain his composure. "But keep in touch so I can send you the money I owe you first time I have any." He studied each face, pale and drawn with shock and sorrow. "We'll take the rest of this day for mourning, but we'll work tomorrow as usual."

A tall, powerfully built man stood and nervously pulled at his grizzled beard. He cleared his throat several times before he could get the words out. "I don't know about the others. Cain't speak fer them. But as fer me, Jonathan, I been at Hartwell Landing since we felled the first tree. You always done right by us in foul times and fair. I'm thinkin' you'll pull us through this one too. I aim to be stayin' on 'til I get planted here."

A young man stood, whom Prudence recognized as having come down from Seattle when she arrived. "Seems to me you been stomped on about as hard as a man can be. Things've got to get better. Can't get no worse. I'm stayin'."

A whoop went up from the group and then each man filed past, shaking Jonathan's hand and promising to stay. Prudence felt small arms grip her leg and she looked into Serena's upturned face. "Does this mean everything's going to be all right?" she asked.

Prudence swiped at her tears and nodded. In her heart, however, she wondered what was to become of her. There was no money to purchase passage for her to leave. This morning Jonathan had been very cool toward her as they went over the books, saying not a word more than he had to. Then, as they finished and she was tidying the desk, she watched him go to the Bible and open it to Anna's picture. He was still holding it and studying her likeness when Prudence slipped silently from the room.

Because there were no bodies to be cared for, no caskets to build, no graves to dig, it was hard to accept the death of the men. But the widows, who were constant reminders of the calamity, left over the next three weeks, so that by the third week of June, the town returned to normal.

During this time Jonathan continued to work himself and his men long hours at top speed to build the inventory. Although a gentle, misty rain fell almost constantly, the dry forest floor absorbed much of it. Even at the edge of the river there was little mud to bog them down.

A steady stream of logs were dragged to a skid that sent them down the mountain and into the river. There came so many floating down to the mill pond, they choked the river. When they jammed against the bank, river pigs ran nimbly over the bobbing trunks and used hooks to break loose the blockage.

Until the last light faded from each lengthening day, the sawmill worked at full capacity. The saws squealed and whined, filling the air with the pungent fragrance of pitch and cedar. The cone-shaped sawdust burner sent an almost continuous plume of smoke up over the trees and away on the wind.

Prudence grew more desperate with each passing day. Most days were cold and misty and she could hide herself under an oversized sweater and full aprons, but soon she would be forced to tell Jonathan of her deceit if she didn't want him observing it for himself. And then she asked herself why she cared if he knew? She had finally understood that he would never marry her, but she was here as his guest and he had a right to know how she came to be in this condition.

Her life settled into an unvarying routine. In the morning she and Serena tidied the house, worked in the vegetable patch, pulling weeds and stretching wire to keep out the deer. In the afternoon Serena went to play with the other children and Prudence worked on the company ledgers. After supper came Serena's bath, storytime, and prayers.

Too tired to do more after Serena was tucked into bed, Prudence sat on the front porch and waited for Hulda to come up from the cook shack. The two women visited a few minutes before going to bed, catching up on the camp news and discussing the little things that separated this day from yesterday and tomorrow.

On a rainy afternoon, about a month after the sinking of the *Anna Hartwell*, Jonathan came pounding up the stairs into the office. Prudence whirled from the chair, dropping her pen in her haste. "What's happened?" She could scarcely speak for the dread that filled her.

Jonathan began stuffing clothes into a canvas bag. "I'm taking the fishing boat to Seattle as soon as I can pack some clothes."

"Jonathan, not Seattle. Not in this storm." Her face compressed with worry.

Jonathan nodded. "The mailboat was just here. Storm's on the way out, he says. And he also said there are three big Chinese junks coming into the Strait. Come to buy lumber is my guess. I can speak some Chinese and I bet I'm the only mill owner who can. I'm on my way to bargain with them. If I can sell the inventory we have, that'll give me money to pay the men and make the first payment to buy my land back. That'll give you money to buy passage to San Francisco when a suitable ship comes in."

Prudence hoped her face didn't reflect her terrible disappointment. She knew he had feelings for her, and she kept hoping some miracle would be worked. She stood rigid while he snapped the bag shut. On his way past her, he picked up the pen and handed it to her. Their fingers touched and the electricity shot up her arm.

"Can I bring you anything from Seattle?" he asked. His

voice seemed a bit unsteady.

"No, thank you," she said softly. "I don't care what the mailboat captain said, I hate having you start out in this storm. You take care, now."

"Don't fret. That captain's never wrong. Besides, in these inland waters, it's safe enough. I'll be fine. I want to get enough money together so you can get out of here." He put on his rain slicker and boots, threw the bag over his shoulder, and was gone.

eleven

Prudence was in the office working on the books when she became aware of the silence. It was deafening and took a minute to get used to. Then it struck her. *The sawmill has shut down in the middle of the afternoon. The saws never stop until dark. What's the matter?*

She threw down her pen and dashed down the stairs. Once outside, she started in the direction of the mill, only to meet Barnabas and his men running toward the dock. There, coming into the Bay, were three Chinese junks, led by Jonathan's fishing boat.

He docked alongside the wharf and motioned for the lead ship to take the loading space. As soon as the Chinese captain came ashore, Jonathan showed him the dry lumber under protective roofs. Each board was carefully stacked with airspaces between to prevent warping and the captain vigorously nodded his approval. Immediately, all millhands, as well as the Chinese crew, began carrying lumber from yard to ship and loading it on board.

When Prudence arrived on the dock, Jonathan rushed to meet her, his face glowing with pride. "They'll take the whole inventory."

Prudence gasped. "That's over seven hundred thousand board feet, Jonathan. That's wonderful. Did you get your price?"

"Just about. I did have to come down a bit." He smiled and shrugged. "These fellows know how to strike a hard bargain. Nevertheless, we'll make enough to bail us out for now." A shout and a wave from Barnabas, and Jonathan hurried off.

Prudence sat on a low piling and watched the men load. Though she sat perfectly still, inside emotions churned like cream going to butter. She was thrilled for Jonathan that he was able to sell the lumber and see enough money to pay his men. He fretted about that night and day. But, it also meant there would be enough money to see her on her way. She could scarcely think about that. She had grown to love this place and, though she fought such thoughts, she knew she loved Jonathan. And of course, Serena had captured her heart in the first moments after her arrival at Hartwell Landing. How could she leave him, them?

Prudence sighed and looked at the low-hung clouds. They didn't need rain to make the loading task any harder than it was. She added a plea for dry weather to her prayer list.

The weather held, and the next day no loggers went into the woods. Every man worked to load the cargo. At the end of the third day, the three ships rode low in the water, their holds stuffed with the best Washington Territory lumber. The Chinese paid in sacks of gold coin and sailed out of the Bay.

It was after dark when she heard the sound of corks on the porch. She opened the door wide to greet Jonathan and Barnabas, each weighed down with money sacks. Jonathan set the record books he carried on the table next to the canvas sacks. "I brought Barnabas along to help us fill the pay envelopes."

"I appreciate your wanting to pay the men as soon as possible, but you both look so tired. Couldn't we do this tomorrow and pay the men the next day?"

"No. Tomorrow's payday and they're going to find something in their envelopes besides scrip. We're paying off a big chunk of our debt, praise God." Jonathan, gray with fatigue, sat at the table and looked in the direction of the stove, kettles still steaming. "We'd feel better if we had some supper. We were settling up with the Chinese captains and missed eating."

Hulda, who had been standing in the doorway to her room, whirled into action and in minutes the table was spread with a delectable meal. After the men finished eating and the table was cleared, Jonathan spread out the record books, envelopes, and money. "Prudence, if you'll make out the payment slips for the men, the rest of us can handle filling the envelopes," Jonathan said and pushed the books in her direction.

It was nearly midnight when the pay envelopes were arranged alphabetically in a box, ready to be handed out in the morning. Barnabas and Hulda excused themselves and now just Prudence and Jonathan remained in the room. Jonathan sank back in his chair and stared into the firelight, his hand wrapped around a sack over half-full of gold coins. Prudence sat in silence across from him, not wanting to speak, to break the closeness that existed between them.

At last, he said, "I know I've mentioned frequently how anxious I am that you leave this place and get on with your life, but I saw the grandest schooner for sale in Seattle. The price is right, and with this money I could make a substantial payment on her and pay the balance when the *Thomas Hartwell* returns from the Orient. If we keep our eyes open, I'm sure we can make some more good sales from the dock...enough to keep us going. But we'll never make as much money as we can selling it to contractors in foreign ports. To do that, we need another ship."

"You do need a replacement boat. This lumber would have brought a fourth again as much if it could have been taken to San Francisco, and a third more if delivered to Hong Kong." Without thinking, she reached across the table and rested her hand on his, the one around the money sack. "Buy your boat, Jonathan. I don't have to leave right away." *I don't have to leave at all, you stubborn man. I don't want to leave and I don't think, if you'd let yourself admit it, that you want me to leave. Why can't we admit that we like each other very much?*

"I have one more favor to ask," he said.

She nodded.

"We're getting timber from high on the mountain. It takes considerable effort to snake it down to the skids and then to the shoot and finally to the river. I'm sure you hadn't thought about cutting on your claim this soon, but as you can see, the mill cuts almost as fast as we can bring down the logs. We could dramatically increase our finished products if we could get the logs down into the pond easier and faster."

"We signed a contract that you could cut on that land any time. Want to look it over in the morning before you leave for Seattle?"

He smiled. "I'd like that."

"What in blue blazes are you doing?" Jonathan shouted from the river where he stood with his hands on his hips.

Prudence looked up from tying a scrap of red yarn around a two-hundred-foot tall Douglas fir. "I've almost finished marking the trees for cutting," she called back.

Jonathan stormed up to where she was cutting another piece of yarn. "What do you mean, marking the trees?"

Prudence sighed with impatience. "Jonathan, you agreed that I would choose the trees you could cut. I'm marking those I've selected."

The anger passed and in its place came a look of complete bafflement. "I fail to understand your motive."

"I've seen what you've done to the other areas you've cut, and you can't butcher this forest like that."

"I'm supposed to bring in a hardened crew of fallers and say, 'You can only cut the trees marked with red yarn'!"

"Yes, Jonathan, you are. You signed the agreement."

"But I didn't think you meant this when you said you would select the trees." He gestured at the traces of red spotted through the woods.

Now it was Prudence's turn to look puzzled. "What did you think I meant?"

"That we'd stake off a certain area to be logged. Pound markers in the ground to show the men where the boundaries were."

"But Jonathan, that's exactly what I don't want. The men would cut down everything inside the stakes."

"But that's the way it's done."

Prudence didn't want to fight with Jonathan. Last night the chill had warmed considerably, but here they were again, just about ready to erupt at each other. "But then I would have a big bare spot in the heart of my forest. Jonathan, I couldn't stand that. After seeing those ugly, denuded hills you leave, I've become a firm believer in selective cutting. That's why I spent every dime I had to buy this land. I wanted to protect this beautiful grove from such treatment."

"There's a lot you don't know about lumbering, Miss Beck. Please allow me to enlighten you." He walked beside her as she continued to cut lengths of yarn and tie them around chosen trees. "What you don't realize is that once a section is clear-cut, the sunshine can get in to the floor of the forest and stimulate the growth of Douglas fir."

He knelt down. "Come, look at this. There are thousands of tiny seeds germinating down in the duff." With his hatchet, he swept away the layers of decaying material to show her how the embryonic trees were taking hold. "But Douglas fir seedlings won't survive in constant shade. They'll die, and the only new trees that will grow to maturity will be the hemlock, which isn't worth nearly as much as cedar and spruce. Even they will be spindly unless the forest is opened up to the light. In the end, you'll lose a profitable operation that can't be replaced in your lifetime."

Prudence stopped in the middle of a knot and stared at him in disbelief. "You're just saying that to justify your cut and run methods."

"What do you mean, *run*? Hartwell Lumber Company bought its land and we expect to log it for years. My grandchildren and their children after them will be receiving the benefits from these forests." His voice shook with emotion.

"I know that my trees will be here to be logged, but I have my doubts about yours."

"That's were you're wrong." He waved his hand toward a giant Sitka spruce. "Some of your best timber will be overaged in ten years. Do you know what'll happen then?"

She stretched to tie a length of yarn around a fine western white pine and didn't answer him.

Jonathan stepped around so she had to face him. "The old trees die and fall down and aren't worth anything as lumber. Overaged trees are targets for disease. Insects burrow in to kill them. You'll end up with a lot of imperfect trees, which make imperfect lumber, which brings in a poor profit."

"Then, explain to me why in Europe. . . ."

"They have hardwood trees in Europe, Prudence. A hardwood forest can't be compared to our trees out here on the Pacific Coast. Our timber trees are softwood. You have to manage them differently."

"Oh, Jonathan, the last thing I want to do is fight with you. But I don't believe you."

"I'll delay my trip and take you to see a selective cut forest and right next to it one that's been clearcut. The clearcut one is already beginning to replenish itself with a sturdy stand of Douglas fir and other fine timber trees. They're all the same age and will reach maturity at the same time. We can log them efficiently and let the cycle repeat again and again. The stand next to it is already showing signs of deterioration."

Prudence wanted to believe him, but when she looked at this perfect stand and thought of the scalped land he left, she shook her head.

He grabbed her arm and marched her deeper into the forest. "Look up there, Prudence. See how your hemlocks are infected with mistletoe. This stand needs to be clearcut to get rid of that parasite. In fact, we ought to cut fifty feet into the healthy trees and stamp it out. If you don't let us, the mistletoe will kill the tops of the trees. Then they'll become perfect conductors for lightening, and you'll lose the whole forest to fire. Mistletoe saps the strength from the trees and they become food for damaging insects. Either way, you've lost your timber."

Prudence felt her exasperation rise and she meant to speak her mind, but prayed she could do it diplomatically. "I guess I don't understand how this forest grew for thousands of years and created this perfect sanctuary all by itself without being managed by anyone. Then, the American lumber man comes and claims that unless he cuts and manages the timber, the trees will grow old, die, and fall down. And the Pacific Coast will be treeless."

She could be the most infuriating woman when she chose. Jonathan gritted his teeth to keep from exploding at her. "No, the Pacific Coast won't be treeless. But Mother Nature has a way of taking care of the problems. A few devastating fires or high winds produce the same effect as clearcutting. The overaged, diseased trees are burned up or blown down and sunlight gets down to the forest floor and the process of rebuilding the forest begins."

He let go of her arm and marched back to the stand of trees she had been marking. Prudence hurried along behind him. "Will you please finish marking the trees we can log. And please keep them close together so we don't have to drag our equipment all over the forest."

Jonathan was highly annoyed with himself for having asked her for her trees. He should have waited until she was gone and come in and cut what he needed. It rankled him badly that she had thought by buying this site she would be helping him. He didn't want her help, didn't want any strings to bind them together. He leaned against the trunk of a Sitka spruce, braced his foot against the bark, and watched her cut and tie those silly pieces of yarn around the trunks of her selected trees.

She cut a length of yarn, raised her arms, encircled the tree, and tied a knot. Snip, tie. Snip, tie. Snip, tie. This was the most ridiculous thing he had watched in ages. His foreman could have chosen much more quickly and equally as well as she. She was one determined woman, he'd learned that much about her. And though she wasn't a beauty, she was a handsome woman—her face serene but intent on her work, her arms shapely. He'd like to see the rest of her, but she was never without that infernal shapeless apron that covered her thoroughly from shoulder to knee.

"Do you think I've chosen enough to keep the men busy while you're gone?" she asked, and looked over for his reaction.

He seemed to reflect the qualities of the Sitka he leaned against. Tall. Substantial. Like the tree, there was strength in him. She had seen it. He could weather the storms life dealt him. But when he thought he was right, he would go to the mat for his beliefs. Right now, that trait was making life hard for both of them. Yet, overall, he was a mighty fine man and Prudence knew she loved him.

Jonathan left the tree and moved alongside her. "You need help. Let me mark some trees for you."

"I don't trust you. You'll mark some I don't want cut."

"I hate to bring this up, but you're marking some extremely poor locations. When they fall they're going to crush too many other good trees. I just might be able to find some with more empty space around them."

She stopped and studied some of her selections. He was right. She hadn't been considering the whole picture when she chose a certain tree. She held out the scissors and yarn to him. "I guess I need some more practice before I go at this alone."

He held up his hand, refusing the scissors. Instead, he took a small hatchet from a leather loop on his belt and made a nick in the bark. "If you don't mind too much, I'd rather do it this way."

"I do mind. If we change our selection, with my way the

tree won't be hurt."

He turned and gave her a disgusted look. "Prudence, I'll be the laughingstock of the whole Sound if I leave your yarn as markers. They're all coming down before we leave."

Prudence trotted to keep up with him. "Now remember, you're only to log near the river. I don't want a lot of skid roads through my forest."

He stopped and looked at her, an eyebrow arched over the squint. "So, now it's your forest. And after all you're fine talk about this being *your* generous act to save the timber here for Hartwell Lumber Company."

Prudence swallowed and thought fast. "What's left is my forest. What's cut is yours, after you pay me. When you log here, I just don't want you to forget the restrictions that are in place."

"I promise to keep in mind all your regulations. Now leave me alone and let me finish. We've wasted far too much time, already. It'll be dark before I get to Seattle."

She sat down on a fallen log and watched him work, swiftly and surely. It was lovely here in the forest, with the summer sun slanting through the trees. In spite of their arguments over the trees, it had been a delightful morning.

Jonathan finished and came toward where she was sitting. She stood to greet him and together they looked over the scene—deep-green conifers silhouetted against a cloudless sky, Mount Rainier in the distant background, a white tumble of water as the river stormed through a rapid above the property and then controlled itself to flow in dainty burbling currents toward the Bay.

Prudence watched in silence as he returned the hatchet to its leather loop, pulled out a large blue bandana and wiped the sheen of sweat from his face. Then, letting her arm sweep across the natural meadow, she said, "You know, Jonathan, this slope would be a perfect place for a house. The view is breathtaking, and it's open enough to see the sun rise in the morning and set in the evening."

The muscles in his jaw flexed, and his gaze shifted eastward, toward the mountain. "You're right. The location is perfect. Anna thought so, too."

Without looking back, he marched down to the river and prepared to launch the dugout canoe.

twelve

In the spring of 1865, the terrible War had been over for a year and Reconstruction was underway. Earlier promises of lumber purchases had turned into signed contracts to buy all the lumber Jonathan could cut and mill. His company was prospering again. In order to keep his experienced loggers and millhands, Jonathan had announced before he left for Seattle that he would arrive home in time for Serena's birthday. On that day he planned to make a present of town lots and sell lumber to the men at half price so they could build permanent homes.

Today was the Fourth of July—the nation's birthday—and Serena's. The day dawned with a warm brightness, as if nature had conspired to make the double event a success. Hulda's husband arrived the day before and anchored his schooner for a lengthy stay, he said. And Jonathan was due any hour now with the new ship to replace the *Anna Hartwell.*

The celebration committee wanted to start the festivities at the wharf and end at the newly designated town square. They planned to have Captain Hartwell's horse saddled and ready so the parade could begin immediately after he disembarked. Prudence, however, asked that they wait until Jonathan could come up to the house and they could have a small private time for Serena to open her presents.

It was shortly after noon when a ship appeared, sails full, at the mouth of the harbor. A cheer went up as she drew near the dock. Lines to snub Jonathan's new schooner

138

tight flew out to waiting hands on the wharf. This ship looked enough like the *Anna Hartwell* to fool all but the most observant, so when Serena began to jump and dance and squeal, "Look, Aunty Prudence, look at the name," few people paid her any mind.

Prudence, whose eyes had been riveted on the grinning figure at the wheel, cast her glance to the bow. There, in bright blue letters, *Serena Hartwell,* stood out against the blinding white of new paint. "Oh, Serena, how wonderful." She hugged the birthday girl and sent a radiant smile in the direction of Serena's thoughtful father.

As soon as the gangplank was in place, Serena dashed into Jonathan's waiting arms. He hoisted her onto his shoulders and carried her down to the wharf. She looked as if she might explode with the joy of it. They stopped in front of Prudence.

"Welcome home," she said. "The *Serena Hartwell* is beautiful. I don't think Serena could have hoped for a better birthday present."

"You think that was all right?" His eyes held questions.

"I think that was better than all right."

"Me, too," Serena echoed.

"Before the parade starts, we have time for Serena to open her other gifts."

"If you two want to go on up to the house, I'll be along in just a few minutes," Jonathan said, and he motioned to Barnabas.

When Jonathan came through the door laden with parcels, Prudence had the small decorated cake sitting in the middle of the table. "What do you want to do first?" he asked Serena. "Open your presents or have cake?"

"Presents!" she announced.

Barnabas had made a bright red stick horse, complete with a red oilcloth head, full mane, and leather reins.

Jonathan brought her a scale model of the *Serena Hartwell*. From Hulda, there were moccasins and a yellow rain slicker that said CAPTAIN on the hat. And Prudence had made her a big rag doll with red hair and wide blue eyes and a complete wardrobe. Serena studied and held each gift, put the schooner in its stand and placed it carefully on the table, put on her moccasins, and decided that the stick horse, which she promptly named Buck, would be wonderful to ride in the parade. She galloped outside to practice.

"I'll save the cake for later," Prudence said. "I think it's an anticlimax to the gifts. The committee is waiting for you to lead the parade. Then, there'll be a picnic at noon, games and races this afternoon, and after dark, fireworks over the water."

"A full day. From the sound of things on the porch, we'd better get started before Buck runs away with Serena."

The children were all in colorful homemade costumes, riding in little carts, on ponies, or on fathers' shoulders. Most of the adults lined the parade route to be an audience. Barnabas, dressed in a red, white, and blue bunting, beat a battered old drum to pace the marchers. After several trips up and down the beach and along the trails that led to the crude slab family houses and split-log bunkhouses, the parade disbanded at the town square. Hungry marchers descended on the tables set under the trees and piled high with mountains of food. When everyone was thoroughly stuffed, the games began. There was a tug of war, a three-legged-race, and a host of contests that kept everyone busy until the last event—the log rolling contest at the pond. At the signal, the river pigs, men who kept the logs floating down the waterway, jumped on logs and ran in place, keeping them spinning at an incredible speed until one by one, the men fell off. The last man still standing won the prize.

Each time a man fell in the water, fully clothed, Serena danced and clapped with delight. "I want to do that," she shouted.

Jonathan laughed and gave her a big hug. "I think you'd better wait until you're a bit older. Why don't you go ride Buck? He looks lonely standing over there by that piling."

She scrambled away and was soon screeching that Indians were coming and everyone better take cover. The pace of the day slowed, and people sat and visited and said they couldn't remember when they'd had a better Fourth.

Prudence set out the last cake while Hulda, her face all aglow, hammered the supper gong and shouted, "Cake and ice cream's ready for the birthday girl."

"Serena will be so excited to have everybody share her birthday cake," Prudence said as she looked for the little girl among the groups sauntering toward the tables. When Prudence didn't see her, she walked to where Jonathan and Barnabas were deep in conversation. "Have either of you any idea where Serena is? I've been icing cakes for the last hour and can't think when I last heard the warning of Indian attacks."

Jonathan and Barnabas looked at each other blankly, then leapt to their feet, eyes wildly scanning the scene.

"She's around here somewhere." Jonathan's voice was unnaturally calm. "Probably galloped up the trail toward the house. I'll check there."

"She liked the log rolling. I'll look that way." Barnabas grabbed some of the single men and they churned off down the beach.

The crowd buzzed with people asking if anyone had seen Serena recently. Children, especially, were questioned, but the answer was always negative.

Jonathan and Barnabas arrived back at the town square

at almost the same time. Neither had seen any trace of Serena.

Immediately the two men organized the loggers and millhands into search teams, each with an assigned area, and they fanned out into the woods. Prudence could feel the knot tighten in her stomach as she tried to imagine where the stick horse might have taken its little rider. She went to the edge of the forest, found the thin twisting furrow Buck had made, and followed it. Several times horse and rider rode to the end of the cleared area, then made a wide turn without entering the dense undergrowth. The trail finally returned to the picnic area and there Prudence lost any continuity.

Tears pricked her eyes and she gave herself a stern dressing down. The last thing needed now was even a hint of hysteria. She stiffened her back and, fighting for control of her emotions, walked slowly along the beach. She forced herself to think the unthinkable and stared into the darkening waters of the bay. Whitecaps were beginning to top the waves and the sea was growing rough enough that if Serena had fallen in, she would be impossible to spot from the shoreline. Prudence couldn't bear to consider but briefly that Serena might have gone to explore her new ship and fallen overboard. Instead, she turned her attention to the rock-strewn beach.

The wind freshened and blew cool, as gray clouds collected in the west. Prudence pulled her shawl around her shoulders and wished for her cloak. But she kept her head bowed, her eyes searching the myriad footprints for telltale signs of Buck's trail.

The farther she went from the center of the recent festivities, the fewer footprints there were, but the clearer the remaining ones became. Finally, the distinctive track of moccasin prints on either side of the thin, irregular line emerged. Prudence's steps quickened as she followed the trail. It led in circles, to all the familiar places and back again, but never did Serena stray from her favorite haunts along the beach. Then, at the log pond in the haste of the search, Buck's furrow and Serena's tracks were destroyed, leaving Prudence with no idea as to which way they had gone.

Standing at the mouth of the river and not knowing where else to look, Prudence turned and walked inland along the thin rocky path upward. The temperature continued to drop, and the sky boiled with dark rain-filled clouds. She pulled the shawl tightly around her shoulders and trekked on.

And then, in the sand bar, she saw the prints and the furrow again. Her heart leapt. But when she tried to shout out her discovery, the wind blew the words away. She would waste precious time and daylight if she tried to locate a search party. No, she would have to go on alone and pray she ran into someone.

Now that Prudence knew Serena had been along the trail, she could see signs between the rocks where the stick horse had scratched the dirt or overturned a stone. What did Serena have in mind, coming out here without telling anyone? Prudence's heart pounded with fear. There were bears in these woods, bears with new cubs. They were most dangerous at this time of year. Jonathan constantly drummed that fact into both Serena and Prudence.

In the dim light she almost missed the signs when Serena turned from the trail and began to climb the steep mountainside.

Dark clouds were so low now they hid the tops of the mountains. In the murky light Prudence set her path beside Serena's up the mountain. The breeze grew stronger until it whipped her skirt and pulled at her hair. She watched the dark clouds thickening overhead and dropping ever lower, and she prayed for enough light to see Serena's ragged trail.

As Prudence climbed she called and paused to listened. But only the thud of her heart, her quick gasp for breath, and the rush of the wind answered.

About midway up the mountain, Prudence, feeling more and more giddy from the sustained effort of the climb, stumbled, lost her balance, and grabbed at a rock for support. She clung to the rock, so light-headed she thought she would surely faint. "Prudence Beck, you can't faint. You can't even consider it. You're the only one who has a chance of finding Serena before dark," she told herself, her voice straining against the mounting storm.

Prudence licked the tip of a dry tongue over dry lips and pushed away from the rock. This was when she felt the pain and the stickiness in her palm. It was a deep puncture wound, the surface of her palm turning an ugly purple, the wound still oozing blood. She made her hand a fist to keep out the dirt, gathered her skirt, and forced herself to go on.

The climb turned into a blur of pain. Her legs ached, her hand ached, her lungs ached, her throat burned, and she longed to give up and go home. However, Serena's wide-eyed, freckled face floated before Prudence, drawing her up the steep slope, and prodding her farther up the mountain.

At the top, giant spruce which sprang from a thick carpet of rotting humus shut out most of the already dim light. Green moss covered the fallen trunks and a dense growth of shrubs fought for any spot the sun shone through. The floor of the forest showed no tracks. Prudence swallowed useless tears and, realizing how easily she could get lost in this wilderness, walked with her left foot on the downhill slope knowing this would take her toward the

Bay.

She stumbled to a halt at the top of sheer, high cliffs rising above the beach. Where had these come from? Not in all her time at Hartwell Landing had she heard any mention of cliffs. She screamed Serena's name, dropped to her knees and peered over the edge. Her heart raced, terrified she would see a crumpled little body far below. Instead, she saw a series of ledges and cracks that made a stairway down the face of the cliff. "Oh, surely Serena, you wouldn't have done anything so foolish as to climb down this cliff," Prudence said aloud. She started to back away from the edge and that's when she spotted it—the bright red of the horse's head, caught in the branches of a small spruce growing just above the high tide line at the foot of the cliff.

Serena's fallen. She's dead. Prudence felt the breath being squeezed from her, her courage wavering. She pressed her eyes shut to the possibility of what she might find. Crouching at the edge of the cliff, she forced herself to search the scene below. There was no sign of Serena. That meant she had deliberately climbed down the natural steps.

The sanest thing to do was to go back to the camp and bring the men, but the tide was already well up. This little cove at the foot of the cliff would soon be cut off from the rest of the beach. If Prudence left now, it would be dark before anyone could return. By boat, finding this small cove in the dark would be difficult, and at high tide there was no beach on which to land.

On the other hand, going down the face of the cliff in daylight was dangerous, but possible. In the dark it would be suicidal. No, there was no way Serena could be rescued until the morning unless Prudence went to her now.

As she walked, her mind touched Bible verses she had

memorized over the years, but nothing seemed to give comfort until she remembered some verses from Proverbs. "Trust in the Lord with all thine heart; and lean not unto thine own understanding. In all thy ways acknowledge him and he shall direct thy paths." A wave of serenity washed through her and calmed her mind.

Yes, Lord, I will trust You to keep Serena safe until I can get down to her, Prudence kept repeating as she studied the direction the rock steps took. Trying not to think what a false step would bring, she eased herself over the cliff into the first footholds. The wind tangled her skirt and seemed determined to tear her from the cliff. "Don't look down, don't look down," she repeated aloud over and over. "The Lord will guide you." She concentrated on her mental picture of the path as she felt for each step with her toes.

Step by step, she made the descent, though she reopened the wound in her palm and left a bloody handprint to mark each step. Even the pain in her palm seemed less when she kept her thoughts on the Lord, crowding out the terror that at any moment she could plunge to her death. The picture of Serena, trapped and frightened out of her wits, kept Prudence moving. Nothing she did or thought, however, changed the pace of her heart. It thundered in her ears, louder than the wind and the sea.

She could scarcely believe it when she reached the rocky base of the cliff. The descent seemed to have taken hours and yet she knew it was only minutes. She shook her head to clear the sudden whirling behind her eyes and looked up through the branches of the gnarled spruce tree again for the bright red of the stick horse. When Buck fell over the cliff, his bridle caught and now he dangled, too high in the tree for Serena to reach. But Prudence lifted him easily from his prison and stood him in some bushes.

She eyed the tide nervously, inspecting the water, the

hard pounding waves rising ever closer to the base of the cliff. Prudence knew she could not climb back up the rock wall, and the tide would soon block the way out of the cove to the beach. Whatever she did, she must be quick or she would be trapped for the night.

Her eyes scanned the surface of the cliff to where it ended in the water. A large clump of shrubs grew out of the face of the cliff, and Prudence moved so she could see around them. There were openings, caves carved over the centuries by the tides. "Serena!" Prudence called and heard her voice echo through the chambers.

Her shoes clattered on the pebbles as she hurried to the entrance, and she could feel the wet sand give under her feet as she stepped inside. "Serena!" she called again. The onrushing sound of the rising tide seemed to swallow her call. She moved into the dark space until the entrance was only a dim glow, the sea a whisper.

Prudence stood rooted in terror. "Serena!" This time her voice was harsh and tinged with hysteria, her breath coming in quick, shallow gasps. In the darkness, the weight and silence of the stone seemed to press down on her. Her blood pounded with a mad rhythm, beating in time to the heart of the mountain. Her ears tuned to tiny rustlings like the sound of insects moving towards her. Prudence forced herself to breathe slowly, deeply.

"Serena, answer me. I know you're in here." Through the rustling Prudence heard a little "meow" like a stray kitten. She crept in the direction of the sound and called again. Again the strange little sound. She kept calling Serena's name, listening intently in the spaces between the echoes of her own voice. The tiny mewlings directed Prudence, but the sounds were so faint she stumbled over Serena in the darkness. The child had cried until she had all but lost her voice.

Prudence pulled the terrified little girl tightly against her, cradling her head against her breast, stroking her damp hair. "Oh, my darling child, it's all right. It's all right. There's a way out. Come now, Serena, we must hurry."

Serena locked her arms around Prudence's neck, little sobs still shaking her body, and refused to let go.

"It's all right. It's all right." Prudence continued to comfort Serena as she carried her back outside and into the twilight.

Prudence was almost mindless with the joy of being freed from the crushing darkness. She drew in deep grateful breaths of the wet, salty air and felt the wind, rain, and sea on her face. "You'll have to walk, baby. It's too dangerous to carry you over these mossy rocks." Prudence grabbed Buck as they went by and using him as a walking stick, together the two of them slipped and slid their way around the rocky point in a race with the tide.

It was fully dark by the time they escaped the reach of the waves breaking on the beach. Serena clutched Prudence's free hand in a death grip as she struggled to keep tired little legs moving. Her voice was only a whisper, so they walked in silence slowly toward the distant lights of Hartwell Landing.

They had walked for what seemed hours and the rain and mist swallowed up the lights toward which they moved. Nothing looked familiar. The water was on the left side, so Prudence knew they were going in the right direction, but the storm was worsening and Serena complained of being cold. Prudence wrapped the shawl around her, but that left Prudence in a light cotton dress which was soaked through. Her teeth began to chatter, and the cold invaded her bones until uncontrollable shivers ran through her. She had no idea how far they were from the wharf when

Serena's steps began to falter.

Prudence knelt and gathered the little girl in her arms. "We're going to pray for help, Serena. I am too tired to carry you and we're both growing dangerously cold. The people from the Landing are looking for us. Our prayers may help to direct them to us. Do you understand?"

Serena nodded her head, wiggled from Prudence's arms, and knelt beside her.

"Dear Lord," Prudence prayed. "You have been our Guardian and Guide this day, and I can't believe You would lead me to Serena and not provide help now that we are at the end of our strength. Please guide those who are searching for Serena. Speak to their hearts and direct them here. Amen."

They both struggled to their feet and resolutely set their faces again toward home. Their progress was slow and painful, and they had gone only a short distance when Prudence felt the child at her side lurch and grab her skirt for balance. Prudence tried and could not pick up Serena and knew the last of her own strength was ebbing. With Serena still clinging tightly, they took slow, irregular steps against the wind. Both of them shivered until Prudence was sure she could hear their bones rattle. With a thin moan Serena stumbled and sank to the ground. Prudence knelt beside the child. "Oh, Serena, what an awful way to end such a glorious birthday," she whispered and let the tears flow. In the dark and rain, Serena would never know that Prudence, too, had given up.

The search crews had combed the forest in every direction from the town, had not seen a single sign, and had come home empty-handed. Jonathan had sent them home to their families and ordered Barnabas to do his nightly maintenance on the saws. Now, in the dark, Jonathan paced the dock, opened his mouth in a mindless scream of agony, and beat his fists on the hull of the *Serena Hartwell*.

And then it hit him like a rock. Not the tide caves, the forbidden tide caves! Had Serena thought because she was five, she could go there? That was the only place they hadn't looked. He raced to the mill to refill lanterns and found Barnabas there, tears streaming down his face, oiling the machinery.

Hands clumsy with fear and cold, they had just finished preparing the lanterns when Hulda came splashing into the mill. "Have you thought of the caves?" she asked.

"I just did," Jonathan said. "We're on our way."

"You'll need dry clothes, food, and rain slickers," she said, and vanished into the night.

In only a few minutes, a couple of the married men arrived, carrying satchels of dry clothing and rain gear for Serena and Prudence. Hulda came running from the cook shack with food wrapped in oiled paper and a rainproof valise. "We're praying," is all she said as she handed Jonathan the food and left to join the solemn-faced adults and silent children making their way into the church room at the back of the sawmill.

The men held the lanterns high and prayed aloud and silently as they picked their way around and over the sharp boulders made slick by the spray of high tide and rain. They rattled the rocks of the beach with their long, purposeful strides. Jonathan led the party, holding his lantern before him as a beacon casting a wide circle of light out over the beach. Even then, he nearly missed the pair. They lay in an unrecognizable heap of sodden cloth against a clump of salt grass above the water line. In the shadows they looked like tangles of seaweed left from the last high tide.

Unconscious, Prudence lay atop Serena, sheltering her and giving the last of her warmth. "Thank you, God,"

Jonathan whispered as he rolled Prudence off.

"Momma!" Serena rasped.

Barnabas picked up the shivering child. Crooning comforting reassurances to her, he wrapped her in blankets and set off for home.

It was too dangerous to carry Prudence, but Jonathan knew if they soon didn't get her warm, she would die. "We'll get her as dry as we can," Jonathan said. He turned to one of the sawyers. "Fetch a stretcher. That's the only safe way to carry Prudence. And hurry!"

"I'll be right back," the man said and left on a dead run through the trees.

Jonathan dried her hair and wrapped her in layers of woolen blankets. While he waited, he held her in his arms as one would a baby, and rocked her and crooned, "It's all right" over and over again.

She snuggled against him. Then, once again her whole body shook with uncontrollable shivers. His arms moved more tightly around her, trying to transfer some of his body heat, some of his strength, to her. Her arms went around his neck and she clung to him, mindless now of all that had gone between them. She felt his lips touch her forehead with unfathomable tenderness, then move to her eyes, her cheeks. "Oh, my beloved Prudence." His voice was rich and gentle. His lips sought hers and met them in infinite tenderness. His embrace, like his kiss, was tender, gentle. His arms held her close to him as if she were a precious object that would shatter if clasped too tightly.

Lights appeared out of the storm and an army arrived. Gentle hands placed Prudence on a makeshift stretcher and rushed her home to the Landing.

Prudence was tucked into her own bed, wrapped in warmed blankets, and surrounded by heated rocks. "Serena?" The question came as a whisper.

"Serena's fine. Just fine," Hulda said.

Prudence sighed. Everything was all right and so she slept. She opened her eyes once to Jonathan's worried frown. Then, utterly exhausted, she slept again.

Prudence slept for twenty-four hours, not even waking fully when she was lifted and urged to drink, though she swallowed the water and broth obediently.

She opened her eyes for a moment and saw Jonathan standing at the doorway. He looked bone weary, his eyes shadowed by gaunt hollows.

She did not know that Ethan had come as soon as he heard. It was he who entertained Serena, held a daily prayer watch for Prudence, kept up the morale of Hartwell Landing.

The next time she awakened, she felt Jonathan's hand touching her forehead, her cheeks. "You're cool to the touch. You're fever's gone. Please wake up so I know you're all right." Jonathan's voice was tense, pleading in his need.

She opened her eyes slowly, blinded by the afternoon sun streaming through her window. She struggled to make her eyes focus. At last, she could see Jonathan clearly, the relief growing in his face. Without thinking, she held out her hand, and without hesitation he placed hers in his. "I'm all right. Please don't worry," she whispered and looked at her hand clenched in his strong warm fist. "Serena! How is Serena?"

Time stilled as she met his searching, compassionate eyes. "She's fine. Gone to help Hulda in the kitchen. How do I ever thank you for risking your life to find her?" he asked. He didn't think this was the time to tell her of the bear teeth marks on the stick horse.

"I can take little credit, Jonathan. I just knew I couldn't stand and do nothing, so I went where no one else had gone.

The Lord directed me the rest of the way."

He drew her hand to his lips, kissing each finger with such tenderness that it brought a lump to her throat. And against her will, tears formed and slid onto her cheeks.

"Come to me," he whispered and she obeyed. He took her hand from his lips and his head bent toward her. She could feel his lips touch her wet face, kissing away the tears. She was embraced by warmth and understanding such as she had never known, knew only that she never wanted to relinquish it. Their lips met in sweet exploration and it was as if no one else in the world, in this place, in this life had ever known such bliss.

As he kissed her, the feelings he felt for her frightened him. The thought of losing her terrified him, but the thought of loving her frightened him equally.

With the resiliency of youth, Serena recovered rapidly and talked freely about her adventure with the bear cub. Jonathan insisted that Prudence, however, have only limited activity. He was right, unfortunately. It seemed she would never get back her strength or be warm again.

At Prudence's insistence, Jonathan brought the books to the house, but he demanded that she only work for short periods of time. Jonathan, on the other hand, worked day and night, it seemed to Prudence. Cutting the trees from Prudence's land increased production measurably. By the middle of July, there was enough lumber cut and sawed to fill the *Serena Hartwell* and there would be enough profit to buy that third ship Jonathan dreamed of.

Jonathan announced he was off to San Francisco and Prudence, though still a bit shaky on the day he was to leave, insisted that she be allowed to walk down to the wharf to kiss him goodbye.

The *Serena Hartwell*, its holds full, rode at anchor low in the water. Barnabas waved at Prudence from the deck as he directed the closing of the main hold door. Everything was in readiness for the departure, but Jonathan was nowhere in sight. Prudence decided to look in the office. Conserving her strength, she climbed the stairs slowly, the sound of her soft steps covered by the screaming saws. She paused on the landing to regain her breath, then stepped into the room. Jonathan was there, and she almost spoke. Her greeting died on her lips, however, when she noticed that his Bible lay open on top of the safe, and he was holding the picture of Anna in his hand. His big shoulders were slumped, his face a mask of grief. Tears streamed down his face as he traced her face, lingering over each feature.

Prudence's delusions shattered. Her hard-won confidence, the soft blossoming of their relationship, all died in those seconds. It was as if spring had never come to her soul. Slowly, as she stood there, winter slipped back into her heart, and she was helpless before the insistence of it.

She must leave.

thirteen

The long dusk of summer had settled over the Bay when Prudence went seeking Barnabas. He was at work on his precious saws. He took one look at her and saw her swaying. "Prudence, you're not strong enough to be out alone," he said, as he quickly sat her on a log and poured her a cup of coffee from the ever present supply on a small wood stove.

"I'm just a bit tired, but I must talk with you, Barnabas. You're the only one who can help me."

He waited in silence for her to continue.

She wrapped her hands around the cup and sipped slowly, buying time and courage. Finally, she framed the words and with a precision that echoed her determination, said, "I must leave Hartwell Landing. Will you help me?"

Barnabas stared at her in disbelief. "Jonathan's finally broken the devil's hold and you are responsible. He cannot take his eyes off you when you are around and mopes when you are not. You will break his heart."

Prudence gave Barnabas a weak smile. "I think not, dear Barnabas. Jonathan would make the arrangements himself when he returns from San Francisco. But, believe me, it will be much better for him, for Serena, if I am gone before they return."

Barnabas felt helpless, but he had to try. "Prudence Beck, I know Jonathan loves you. He has told me so and surely, he has told you in every way but words. And I know you love him. What more is there than that?"

"Yes, Barnabas, I love him, but that's not enough. There are things he....you don't know. Jonathan deserves better than me. He deserves someone like Anna."

"Anna is dead!"

"Not for Jonathan." A thick silence hung between them. "Please, Barnabas, grant my request. If not for me, then for him."

Barnabas bowed his head. He loved Jonathan like a brother, and he had grown fond of Prudence, too. This was Ethan's problem and rightfully, he should solve it. He, however, had his own timetable and could not be counted on. She was so alone and so far from home, and there was no one else but him to help her. He could not forsake her in her need. "There is a good ship sailing from Seattle in three days. I know the captain. He will take you."

"I can pay the passage."

He nodded curtly. "Be here just before dawn of the day after tomorrow. Will you tell Hulda and all the people who have come to love you?"

"No, it would serve no purpose. They will all know soon enough."

Through that day and the day after, Prudence clung to reality with a fierce grip. However, vivid images became a part of each hour. Jonathan caressing Anna's photograph haunted her. Memories made with Jonathan and the promises of what might have been engulfed her. The need to cuddle Serena grew to a physical ache.

Night and darkness of the second day finally arrived. At Prudence's insistance, Hulda went to sleep on board her husband's ship, and Ethan begged that Serena be allowed to accompany him on a week's trip to conduct church services at a new settlement on the peninsula.

Now, beyond the clothes for the baby, Prudence packed

very little. What she left behind could be sold or given to the logger's families.

She went to Jonathan's room, intending to leave letters for him and Serena. The Bible and picture were gone. For a long time, she stared at the empty table beside his bed. Heartbroken, she didn't write anything. There was nothing to say. Jonathan would be relieved to have her gone. Serena would not be assuaged by any words on paper. If she didn't understand the depth of Prudence's caring now, words wouldn't make that clear.

There was nothing to do except wait for the time to pass. She didn't try to sleep. She went, instead, to Serena's room. Everything was in order. Hulda had cleaned it as soon as Serena left, but there was still the scent of her, the faint wild earthy fragrance that clung to her and no amount of bathing removed.

"Sleep well, Serena," she whispered, just as if she were there.

The clock struck the hour before dawn, and Prudence, hoping she wouldn't be seen by any early risers, set out for the sawmill. The night was moonless and she carried no lantern as she walked the familiar path, trusting herself to remember the twists and turns, the irregular rises and exposed roots that threatened to trip one even in strong daylight. A damp mist blew against her and the coldness seemed to seep into her heart.

Barnabas was waiting for her, his face set and grim. "What you do is not good. You will not change your mind?"

"No, and you?"

"I promised, and I will take you."

In the purple light of beginning dawn she watched the sawmill and Jonathan's house on the hill grow smaller as they sailed west out of the bay, the freshening wind working in the sails of the lugger. And then they turned north and she forced herself to look away, away from the place her heart told her was home.

It was a dismal journey. The wind grew stronger, and the cold wetness of the salt air stung Prudence's face until she wrapped a scarf around for protection. Barnabas, his hand steady on the tiller, showed no concern with the cold, but neither was he interested in talking. He had said all he had to say on the wharf. Now he demonstrated his disapproval as he stiffened his back and turned from her. The silence hung between them, more daunting than the gray, windy weather.

A pallid sun broke through late in the morning, and in the early evening, they sailed into Seattle's harbor. Prudence had forgotten what a dreary, ramshackle little town it was.

She was cold and stiff and wanted nothing more than to crawl into a warm bed. Barnabas took her arm and she went silently and meekly where he led. He turned in at the wharf-side saloon frequented by seamen, and through the dim, smoky interior found the captain at his favorite table.

He rose abruptly when he saw Barnabas had a woman with him. "Why, Miss Beck, or is it Mrs. Hartwell now? What might ye be about that ye need my services?"

"Captain Sperry, what a surprise," Prudence managed to say and pressed a smile on her face. She looked at Barnabas' innocent face and knew he had deliberately waited until Captain Sperry's ship was available before bringing her to Seattle.

Captain Sperry still stood, so Prudence slid quickly into the chair he indicated. "Miss Beck it still is," she said and hoped her voice sounded reasonably normal. Then, to

Barnabas, "How prophetic, I came on the *Tanner* and I leave on her as well." Her voice was musical with sweetness, but her eyes flashed her distress. How could he put her in the hands of one who would report back to Jonathan at the first opportunity? Stoic as Barnabas normally was, he colored under her questioning gaze.

Satisfied that Barnabas understood that she knew what he had done, Prudence said to Captain Sperry, "It is necessary for me to receive medical attention in San Francisco before I return to care for my mother in the East."

The captain made appropriate noises of sympathy that Prudence's long journey had ended so sadly even while he named the fare to San Francisco. His eyes regarded her calmly, with no pity or warmth marring their cool gray. Captain Sperry would tell Jonathan nothing of her passsage. Everything was on a business level. Could she please be aboard promptly at seven the next morning? She could.

Once outside again, Barnabas said curtly, "You'll have to spend the night at a hotel." Coins jingled as he pulled out a leather pouch.

Prudence was taken aback at his generous offer. However, she said, "Put it away, Barnabas, though I thank you. I have enough to manage." She thought of the schooner loaded with lumber, her lumber, on its way to San Francisco to make money for the purchase of a new ship. And she thought of Jonathan, always of Jonathan, standing like he was king of the world at the helm of the ship bought with money from the sale of Prudence's timber. At least she had made the down payment on the new schooner even though he planned to name her the *Anna Hartwell II*. Prudence had heard him tell Serena as much, and her heart wrenched at the news. It was only then she realized she secretly hoped he would name the ship after her. Would she never recover her good sense when it came to Jonathan?

Barnbas led her to a well-kept building which looked most respectable. He set her bags down and nodded toward the entrance. "Go in and make sure they have a room for you. Tell them you're sailing on the *Tanner* in the morning. And act like you're rich and could buy the hotel so the clerk won't think your a. . .a. . .lady of the evening come for a few hours."

Prudence turned icy. He wasn't leaving her alone? She wasn't ready for that just yet. "What about you?" she asked, her voice trembling despite her best efforts to control it. "Where will you be staying?"

He shook his head, and his voice was brusque. "Back at the Landing they'll be frantic about you. I'm the only one who can tell them you're safe. Don't worry, a dark sea is no stranger to me."

He disappeared into the night mist before she could frame an appropriate sentence to thank him for all he had done for her.

Her face was so severe, her manner so haughty when she asked for a room, the clerk didn't think of refusing her and asked timidly about her baggage. "It's outside, and I do not need assistance with it," she told him, taking her key, turning on her heel, and leaving him drop-jawed to wonder who she was and what her business was.

She bent to pick up the bags when his hand closed over hers. "There's still time to work things out. Come back with me." Barnabas' voice, deep and rolling like the sea, pierced her after the long, cold day.

"Jonathan and I were doomed before we ever met. I pretended it would work if I tried hard enough. But lies, deceits, and a love that won't ever dim make it impossible to pretend any longer. Care for Jonathan, care for him as you always have, and for Serena." She drew a deep shuddering breath. "What am I saying? Of course you will care for them because you love them as I do. And...." She paused until she swallowed the tears. "And when you think of me, if you ever should, please think of me with kindness. Please, Barnabas."

She wanted to, but was afraid to touch him. It was his strong arms that drew her close. "I could never think of you with less than kindness, Prudence Beck. You lit up the lives of all of us at the Landing. Fair winds." He released her abruptly and did not look back.

The swell of pain crushing her chest was beyond tears. Never had she wanted anything so desperately as to be home in Hartwell Landing. Home with Jonathan and Serena. But she did not follow nor call Barnabas back.

Though their time together had been short, Prudence and Jonathan had shared so much. Little things and big, the kind that build a relationship, bind people together and forever change them. She had left a vital part of herself at Hartwell Landing, and she knew that though time would dull the pain, she would always feel incomplete.

The voyage from Seattle to San Francisco became a blurred memory of cold misery—cold sea air and a deeper cold within that congealed all feeling. It became even worse when sudden shafts of clear remembrance pierced through the fog—the sound of Serena's voice and laughter; Hulda showing Prudence how to prepare an exotic dish; and Jonathan. Her mind played tricks with him. Sometimes he seemed never to have existed and she could not see him clearly. Then he would be everywhere at once, his voice ringing in her ears, the clean, earthy smell of him permeating the cabin, the hard muscles of his arm rippling under her fingers, the taste of his kiss lingering on her lips. From the sharp edges of this image, pain flooded her until she thought she would die.

Once in San Francisco, Captain Sperry offered his assistance in obtaining her passage on to the East, or...and he looked directly at her ballooning shape, he would be glad to assist with a place to live and perhaps some light work she could do. However, Prudence had no intention of going anywhere just now. It was less than two months before she calculated her baby was due, and she dare not risk anything more. She wanted no one remotely connected with Hartwell Landing to know her whereabouts, so she graciously declined his offer, permitting him only to hail her a hansom cab, place her luggage aboard, and murmur something to the driver.

The hotel in Seattle and her passage to San Francisco had taken almost all her pitifully small store of money. She had not thought clearly about anything except the need to leave Hartwell Landing, to leave Jonathan at the earliest possible minute. When he could spare enough money to pay some of her back salary, she knew the time had come for her to go.

Now, however, she had to face the reality of what she had done. She had been prideful and stubborn in refusing Barnabas' offer of the coins and Captain Sperry's assistance. She barely had enough to pay for one week at Kate Mulhroon's boarding house.

Prudence needed a job, needed it desperately. Though sewing paid poorly, it was the only thing she was able to do right now. If Kate Mulhroon would believe and trust her, Prudence would sign a note for what the sewing didn't pay. When Jonathan sold the next boatload of lumber, she could and would pay the debt. But Kate, short and stout, wasn't in business for her health. She had said so on their first meeting when she saw Prudence's flat purse. And there wasn't the slightest hint of a smile on Kate's round, deceptively jolly-looking face to take the sting from her words.

It took three days for Prudence to gather her courage. Even then, she was trembling and hoping it didn't show as she approached Kate with her proposal. Prudence entered the small back room Kate used as an office and found her standing in front of a huge rolltop desk. Kate, hands on her hips and a look of bewilderment distorting her normally placid features, stared at a mountainous jumble of papers. Some had even spilled onto the floor when she opened the desk.

"Have I come at a bad time?" Prudence asked in a voice strangled by fear of Kate's reaction.

At Prudence's question, Kate whirled and backed against the desk, spreading her skirts to hide the overflowing contents. "What do you mean, sneaking up on a body?" Her voice was cold as ice and not a blush burned her face.

"I. . .I. . .am truly sorry to have startled you, but I did knock."

"If you did, I suspect it was with a feather, else I'd have heard you."

The mood wasn't good for requesting a favor of Kate, but Prudence was desperate. Without waiting for Kate's permission, Prudence moved into the room. Her foot kicked one of the slips of paper and she bent to pick it up. As she handed it back to Kate, she noticed it was a signed receipt for a month's board and room. The date was August, 1863. Prudence picked up several more papers from the floor. Each was in a different handwriting.

"Kate, are all these slips of paper receipts for money

paid you?"

Kate nodded. "Not that it's any of your business, girl." Kate's voice was gruff as she tried to stare down Prudence.

Kate's obvious discomfort made Prudence bold and she didn't blink. "How far behind are you in your bookkeeping?" Prudence asked.

Kate stood silently smoothing her apron.

"Where's your ledger, Kate? In exchange for my room and board, I'll get your books caught up and keep them caught up."

"You can do that?"

"I can and I will, and when I've finished, I'll sew for you. Mend your sheets, your towels, make you new towels and sheets. Sew you some new dresses if you'll but buy the fabric." Prudence stood, hope beating fresh in her breast, praying Kate would agree to her propositon.

Kate ran a rough hand over her faded gingham dress. "Been a long time since I had me a new dress. My husband being lost at sea took the heart right outta me."

"We have an arrangement, then?" Prudence held her breath.

Kate nodded and a crooked smile creased her face.

Prudence pulled up a chair and immediately began the tedious job of separating the slips by years and months.

Working eight hours a day six days a week, it took Prudence well into August to complete Kate's ledgers. She found foreign coins, uncollected scrip, promissory notes, and jewelry both worthless and of unknown value. Every drawer and niche of the desk was stuffed. When asked about her bank account, Kate snorted and said she didn't believe in banks. Prudence took it upon herself to make application for a bank account and brought home the signature card for Kate to sign.

Now, as Prudence closed the final ledger and patted it, she remembered that moment as vividly as the day it happened. Kate found all manner of excuses for not signing until Prudence finally realized that Kate couldn't read or write.

"Oh, Kate, why didn't you just tell me?" Prudence hugged the embarrassed woman.

"You got no idea what a mortification it is not even to be able to sign your name. My dear departed husband always took care of all those things. When he passed on, I had the house and I could cook, so I started renting rooms and taking in boarders. With the big garden and bottling everything I could, I didn't need much money. Just enough for staples. What wasn't American gold coins I stuffed in his desk. You was a Godsend, Miss Prudence Beck. A real answer to prayer."

Prudence winced at Kate's use of the word, 'Miss' and promised herself she would tell Kate that very day about the baby. Instead, she had said, "Well, you're going to learn to sign your name immediately, and then I'll teach you how to read and write."

Now, as Prudence sat down to do the day's books, the baby gave a powerful kick as though to remind Prudence she hadn't said a word to Kate about the impending birth. If she waited any longer, there would be no need of words. Each day she seemed to balloon more until she had to set even wider gussets in the waists of her dresses and add gathered inserts in the aprons she hid behind.

Oh, Jonathan, I miss you desperately. And Serena. What are you both doing? Do you ever think of me, even briefly? I'm so frightened and lonely. I don't want to spend the rest of my life without you, trying to raise a child without a father. Because, you see, Jonathan, you've spoiled me for any other man. What a pitiful pair we are. Your heart aches with loneliness for Anna so that you can see no other. And mine aches for you with a permanency I know will mellow but never leave.

She sighed and forced her thoughts back to the books. The effort was futile, however, and she closed the ledger. She had just shut the top on the desk when Kate bustled in from the kitchen.

"Are you starting the books or finishing?" she asked.

"Neither. I think I'll wait until later. I have a hem to put in for your friend. She said she'd be by before noon."

This morning, as Kate now did daily, she stood before the chevalier mirror and put on her stylish new bonnet, her smart cape designed by Prudence, then with a flourish dropped a small, satin drawstring pouch into her tapestry bag. As Kate prepared to go shopping, she praised Prudence for her efficiency at book work and her skill as a seamstress.

The door clicked shut and Prudence tried to settle down to her sewing. However, there was a persistent ache in her lower back and she felt heavy and tired. Ever so briefly the thought crossed her mind that the baby might be about to come. She stitched from memory and let her mind drift, wondering if she would have a boy or a girl. If it were a girl, she hoped it would look like her beautiful sisters. What fun it would be to sew elegant gowns for a daughter. She would begin with a most elaborate christening dress.

And then she let her thoughts run riot. Jonathan standing by her side at their daughter's christening. Jonathan— holding the most beautiful girl child in the territory. Jonathan—beaming from ear to ear the smile of a proud father. Jonathan—turning soft, misty eyes on her, Prudence, and letting them tell her how much he loved her.

It happened swiftly, and Prudence was taken completely by surprise. The front door opened and closed, and heavy footsteps came down the hallway and into the kitchen. Dimly, Prudence concluded that Kate had returned and kept on with her work.

"Prudence Beck, I know you're somewhere in this house. Are you going to come out willingly or do I tear the place apart until I find you?" the voice roared from the kitchen.

She froze, her hand suspended in mid-stitch, unable to move, her body rigid, her eyes unfocused. Though the house had been far from noisy, suddenly it took on an eerie silence. Not a board creaked, even the caged canary in the kitchen stopped singing. Prudence knew nothing at all except that Jonathan was here.

She sat motionless for a moment more, then she stood and walked with firm steps to the doorway, but her heart skipped beats. *Prudence, he has only come to give you your payment for lumber. He loves Anna. He will always love Anna. Never forget that fact for a moment, else you will look the fool.* But her heart said he had come for her, Prudence. That's what her heart said.

Fire moved and gleamed in Jonathan's eyes. For whatever reason, the Captain had come to claim what he deemed his own.

"Well, do I drag you out of here or do you come on your own?" His voice was soft, deadly now.

Over his shoulder, Prudence saw Kate move from the pantry into the kitchen, a cast iron skillet poised over her head. "No, Kate!" she cried. "It's all right. This is Jonathan Hartwell. He'll do me no harm."

"That is not a safe conclusion to draw," he snapped. "What possessed you to leave the way you did?" They stood before each other, hands at their sides clenched into fists like combatants ready to square off in a fight. He reached and grabbed her arm. "Where can we talk in private?"

She pointed over her head and did not resist as he pulled her down the main hall. The journey up the stairs seemed endless, but when they got there, she withdrew from him and put as much distance between them as the small space allowed. There was only a small curtained window, and fog absorbed much of the afternoon light. Her hand shook as she lit a lamp.

The fear and agony of loss that had built in Jonathan ever since he discovered her gone drained slowly away. He was so relieved to find her after searching so desperately, that he was torn between the desire to spank her as he would a disobedient child and the urge to fold her into his arms and hold her there forever. And so he remained unmoving just inside the doorway, glaring at her.

"You're the worst kind of thief," he growled.

Her throat constricted and her mouth framed his name silently and then she found a voice, a stranger's voice, a small tremor of sound not like her own at all. "I don't understand. I took nothing but the barest of necessities and the money you paid me for my lumber. Surely you know I wouldn't touch the money in the safe!"

She was caught in an unending nightmare, unable to waken, and it was worse than knowing she would never see him again. She stumbled to her sewing basket. Her hands groped blindly and came up with a small chamois bag, fumbled to untie it. Coins clinked together as she poured them into her palm.

"Did my lumber not sell for the price you thought?" She held out the coins. "These were to pay my board and room, but Kate will wait. You take them. It's all I have now, but if it isn't enough, tell me what you think I owe, and I'll send it when I have it." Her voice no longer trembled and her hand held steady. She felt her body, her heart, her soul, turn to hard, cold metal like the coins. Jonathan looked around the clean, sparsely furnished little room and at her face, pale and hollow-eyed—a remembrance of how she looked when she arrived in his life—and he knew the effort the pitiful little hoard of coins had cost her. A great knot filled his throat and made his voice ragged.

"I'm not talking about money in the safe or lumber profit. Great grief, woman! You took other things without permission. Things I can't afford to lose."

She clung to the table, staring stupidly at him, unable to comprehend what it was he meant and thus unable to form an intelligent answer.

He crossed the space between them in two long strides and gripped her shoulders. She tried to shrink away, but he held her, his long fingers biting into her flesh. "You took my trust, Serena's trust. You took our joy in life, our love. You took most of my heart and a great portion of my soul, far more than I can spare."

Roughly, he pulled her to him and coins clinked across the white painted floor.

"What are you talking about?" she cried. "About the hurt to Serena, I admit guilt and have prayed constantly for her forgiveness. But you, Jonathan, you gave me dregs and them only once. After you led me to believe you cared for me, I saw you studying Anna's picture, tracing her face, and wiping at the flow of tears. I knew then I was only the stand-in for her when your need to love her grew too great to contain. Jonathan, I will never be more than that in your heart or your soul. I know that now, and I'm willing to accept it."

Jonathan sighed softly, his anger and despair lifting with the reassuring press of her against him. He sat down and pulled her onto his lap. "My lovely lady, I studied Anna's picture, took it with me on the schooner, because I could no longer remember what her face looked like. When I thought of her, it was your face I saw, your voice I heard, your lips I tasted. On that trip to San Francisco, I finally understood what Anna has been trying to tell me for years. I wept for the joy of knowing freedom from the ache in my heart. From that photograph she smiled her blessing on us both, gave me permission to love you, to marry you." He held her more tightly. "When I returned to tell you how much I loved you and wanted to marry you and found you gone, I nearly lost my mind. It was like going through Anna's death all over again."

His arm rested across her stomach and when the baby kicked, her blood ran cold, all color drained from her face. She made no sound beyond the first gasp and stared in wide-eyed mortification at him. I must tell him and now. I must!

His relief that she made no struggle to free herself from his hold caused him to almost miss the whispered words. "I came to you pregnant with another man's child." A great shuddering sob escaped her.

fourteen

Jonathan searched for something appropriate to say to Prudence who sat with her head bent as though in prayer, and her hands clasped until the knuckles whitened. She began to speak in an almost inaudible voice, the words forced out in short, painful sentences. "Living out here, it's impossible to understand what the east is like after the war. So many men were killed. So many of those who were single and not injured too severely fled west. Anything to forget the horrors they had been through. A place to start a new life. I fell victim to a zealous do-gooder. He saw a wonderful opportunity to feather his own nest and save us plain ones from spinsterhood."

She shifted in the chair, the penitent bearing disappeared and she looked squarely at Jonathan as she said, "I'm willing to do almost anything to keep my baby from bearing ridicule and scorn, Jonathan. Do you understand that?"

"I do now," he said softly.

"Oh, Jonathan, day after day I tried to tell you, but there never seemed a right time. The months slipped by, and I grew more panicky. Finally, I concluded there never would be a right time. After the Fourth of July celebration and you kissed me, I had every intention of telling you.

"I came up to your office for that very purpose when I found you weeping over Anna's picture. I understood then that the kiss had been an emotion of the moment, a reaction to your relief that I had found Serena. I realized that there

171

was nothing I could do that would make any difference. You would always love Anna. There would never be room in your heart for more than friendship for me. That's when I knew I had to leave.

"After you sailed, I persuaded Barnabas to help me. He argued and pleaded for me to wait until you came back, but in the end, knowing I would go with or without his help, he took me to Seattle and made the arrangements for me to come to San Francisco.

"My plans now are to have the baby and go home to live with my mother. It will be a simple matter to tell the people in Tyngsboro that my husband had been killed in a mine, or something."

She pulled herself out of the chair and staggered toward the doorway. Jonathan's strong arms caught her as she swayed and crumpled. He half-carried, half-led her back to the chair. She turned her back to him and, helplessly, he watched wretching sobs shake her body.

"Prudence," he said gently, "I've know since the night you shaved me that you were with child. At first I was angry, angrier than I can ever remember being, as I waited for you to tell me. And you didn't. Then, I began to fall in love with you, and I grew more and more frightened about the baby. You see, there's something only Ethan knows, and I doubt he ever thinks of it. He's my half-brother. My mother died when I was born." He inhaled a quivering breath. "I've always wondered if I killed her." The stark words were soft and shaky. "Then, when my Anna died the same way, I couldn't even begin to deal with it."

Prudence drew him into her arms, speaking to him as she would a little child. "You know it's not the mother's fault and it's not the baby's either. It just happens."

"Don't you see? The more I cared for you the more the idea of your bearing a child filled me with gut-wrenching fear. It matters so much now because you matter more, so much more. And all I can think is that you will die, too, and I can't bear to have that happen. Never again can I live through that nightmare."

"Jonathan, I've been to the doctor. I'm healthy. The baby is strong, but small. It has another six weeks to fatten up, though. Everything is just fine." She sat forward to ease the dull ache in her lower back.

"Well, I suppose you and the doctor should know. I'll trust you. But we have another matter that needs to be taken care of immediately." Jonathan slid to one knee before her and very formally asked, "Miss Prudence Beck, would you do me the honor of becoming my wife?"

Now that he had asked the question, which only three months ago she would have given all she had to hear, she hesitated. "I'm not Anna. I can never come close to being her. And she is still such a part of your life, you keep her picture in your Bible. It was to her you went when Serena was found." She fought back the tears. "It was *her* face you traced with your fingertip after you kissed *me*." Her voice faded into nothingness.

"Look at me, Prudence Beck, and listen carefully. You didn't see what you thought you did. Anna was beautiful, and I loved her. But that night before I sailed, for the first time I realized, really realized, how long it had been since Anna died. I hadn't loved anyone since, hadn't even felt alive since her death. Life was easier that way. Not good, but easier. And then you came into my life and brought back the past with all its emotions—feeling alive again, loving again, putting everything at risk again. I was afraid, plain and simple. But then on Serena's birthday when I saw how she clung to you and called you Momma, I realized how sad and angry Anna would have been with my mourning. Deprived of her mother, I deprived our child of my love. That day I finally accepted that Anna was gone and so was the young man who had loved her.

"I should have told you then that I loved you. My dearest Prudence, have I waited too long?"

Her face was very still for a moment, then she smiled. "No, Jonathan, I believe this was well-timed. I would be proud to be your wife." She was glowing so brightly with love that Jonathan felt he was surrounded by sunlight.

Eyes met eyes, all wariness gone.

His were clearer than she had ever seen them and filled with emotions that at once frightened and elated her.

Hers were green pools of emotion and longing and warmth.

Her hand moved in his palm, and she wondered at its hard, calloused strength that disguised such gentleness. She traced the lines with love, her eyes never leaving his, being pulled ever deeper into the whirling depths she saw there, watching as each movement of her hand created new golden lights.

A muscle twitched in his face as he resisted the desire the grab her and hold her tight. This must be her decision. She must come to him. And she did.

Her hands moved to his face, to the lines so deep for one his age, and her fingertips sought to ease the pain engraved there.

Shyly, she leaned forward and slid her arms around his neck and kissed him, gently at first and when he responded, the kiss overflowed with the love that had grown between them.

As Prudence stood with Jonathan before Ethan, she felt the strength and calm of Jonathan's voice surround her, warm her, but she had a moment of panic as she feared she was imagining, as she had so often, this moment and doubted she would be able to speak. Then, she heard her own voice, as steady as Jonathan's, as steady as Barnabas' when he gave her into Jonathan's keeping.

"I, Prudence, take thee, Jonathan, to be my wedded Husband, to have and to hold from this day forward, for better for worse, for richer for poorer, in sickness and in health, to love, cherish, and to obey, till death us do part, according to God's holy ordinance; and thereto I give thee my troth."

Ethan's voice drifted over them, "Bless, O Lord this ring. . . ."

Kate, Ethan, Barnabas, and the women who lived in the house—Prudence could feel their love filling the flower-bedecked sitting room. What a twenty-four hours it had been! Prudence had been allowed to do nothing. Kate and the women decorated the room, planned the supper to follow, and dressed the bride. Ethan and Jonathan had taken care of the details.

Now, Jonathan took her left hand. "With this ring I thee wed: In the name of the Father, and of the Son, and of the Holy Ghost. Amen."

The wide gold band warm from Barnabas' hand fit perfectly, though it was the first time Prudence had seen it. Ethan's face radiated serenity and joy. His smile said he had known all the time that things would work out.

When Ethan pronounced the final blessing, Jonathan bent to kiss Prudence. He smelled the tiny roses in her hair, saw the golden light glowing in her green eyes before she closed them, felt her mouth warm and trembling under his own, and forgot there was anyone else in the room.

Ethan cleared his throat and said clearly, "May I be the first to extend my felicitations to you, Mrs. Hartwell." And he hugged them both.

Though Prudence ate little, she joined in the chatter and laughter during supper. But her attention was mainly on Jonathan. She reached out to touch him now and then, assuring that herself this all was real, that he was really here beside her, that they were well and truly married. Each time when she turned to look at him, she found him observing her, bright warm light moving in his eyes.

Suddenly, she wanted them to be alone. Jonathan had suggested they stay in a hotel, but Prudence, with no logical reason, had wanted them to spend their first night of married life in her room here at Kate's. She felt the blush touch her cheek as she wished the carriage would come to take Ethan and Barnabas to their hotel rooms.

She felt the eyes of all at the table on her, smiled at them and sat tall in an effort to relieve the throbbing in her lower back. But the act only seemed to deepen the pain.

"Ethan, don't you think it's getting late?" Jonathan asked hopefully.

Ethan fumbled for his watch. "It's only seven. Not late to my way of thinking."

Kate pushed her chair from the table, stood and glared at Ethan. "Men can be dense beyond belief sometimes. Come, ladies. We'll help these men find their way to their hotel and let Prudence and Jonathan have a few hours alone." She looked hard at Ethan. "Unless, of course, you have some objection, Preacher."

Ethan blushed and stammered, "I agree completely, Kate. Come Barnabas, let's find a cab while the ladies take a minute to primp and get their cloaks."

Jonathan and Prudence waved goodby and shut the door. It was then a sharp cramp made her wince. It couldn't be? It was too early.

Everything turned into a blur. She clamped her teeth together, but she couldn't stop shivering.

"What is it, sweetheart?" Jonathan cradled her hands. "Your hands are icy. Are you ill?"

"I think perhaps I need to lie down."

She had no breath for talking. She clung to Jonathan on the silent ascent to her room, their room.

The door closed behind them and Jonathan led her to the bed. "I think there's been too much excitement for your good," he said. "You'll be fine after you've had a rest." He pulled off her shoes and then his own. He bunched the pillows into a cozy nest and lay down beside her, cradling her in his arms. "Better?" he asked.

Prudence laid her hand on her stomach. "I don't believe anything is going to make me feel better. I fear this little one may be thinking about joining us a bit sooner than we thought."

He pulled away from her and she watched his face flatten as if she'd struck him with a skillet. "Prudence, are you sure? I mean, it isn't time."

"Yes, I'm sure. Babies can't tell time. They come when they've a mind to."

His brow furrowed and the tempo of his breathing changed dramatically. His growing panic was painfully obvious. "Prudence, there's nobody here. Wha...what do you want me to do?"

"Nothing, except stay with me and hold me. Kate and the others will be back in time, I'm sure."

"Of course they will." He forced himself to relax and wondered briefly why he thought he might have to do more than pace the floor.

Jonathan kissed her and held her until she fell asleep in his arms. With Prudence legally his wife, he could finally admit the truth. He had loved her even as far back as the day she came to Hartwell Landing, a water-logged, exhausted woman with an indomitable spirit which nothing seemed to quench.

She stirred and uttered a little moan in her sleep. He rubbed her back and murmured to her until she grew quiet and again, relaxed against him.

Wide awake, in his mind's eye he saw Anna with more accuracy than he had in all the years since her death. He heard the mellow, bubbling sound of her laughter. He saw her look at him from under shuttered lashes, her way of sharing a complaint. He saw her radiance when she knew she would bear his child and, beyond wanting him, wanted it more than anything in the world. He saw the tranquil paleness of her face in death.

And for the first time he also saw clearly how his inability to let go what was gone had caused the long, poisonous course of his mourning.

"Bride of my youth, I did love you so!" The words were only in his head, but he saw the flash of Anna's answering smile, heard her laughter again, and felt the healing knowledge that at the moment she died, she had wished him well and let him go. The monument of sorrow and regret was the most unfitting tribute he could have given her. He let tears fall for Anna, the first he had shed for her and the last he would ever allow himself.

Anna, who had cried easily and as easily stopped, had been impatient with his repugnance of tears. "My dauntless man, tears are the rain of the soul. They are meant to wash you clean and make you grow. If you don't let them out, you'll slowly drown inside."

He remembered exactly how she tilted her head and laughed with the tears still glistening on her cheeks. That lovely last image faded into the reality of Prudence sleeping in his arms. This one, this precious one, seldom shed tears, quietly kept her agonies locked inside. Men had not been kind to her. It would take time for her to completely trust him, trust the realness of his love. He could not push her or, even though they were married, she would bolt again. This was the price they both would have to pay for his pernicious grief. He set about planning how he would make love a part of their shared life, planning it as carefully as he did his business goals. In her sleep Prudence squirmed and protested against the sudden discomfort as he held her too tightly.

He eased his hold. "My own love, my precious love," he whispered as he settled into sleep beside her.

In the early morning hours it became apparent that this was not a false alarm. The baby was coming early.

"Don't go anywhere," Jonathan said, as he lit the lantern. His hand shook so he could scarcely accomplish the task. "I'll go fetch Kate."

Prudence laughed. "I plan on staying right here."

Jonathan fled out the door, his pounding footfalls echoing down the hall. Doors slammed, feet sounded on the stairs, first down, then up. He reappeared wild-eyed in their bedroom. "There's nobody here. They must have all stayed at the hotel. Prudence, is it too late to go for Kate? Don't answer. I can't, I won't leave you alone."

Prudence watched the fear in his eyes and made her voice light, conversational. "I'll fix the bed while you start heating water."

"*I'll* fix the bed and start heating water. Where are the

bedclothes?"

"It's best if I move around, but it's probably not wise to try the stairs. You set the water to heat. We need both hot and cold on hand."

"Move around if you like, but I'll do the bed, just tell me how!" Then, he raced downstairs and she heard water splash from the pump into a bucket and then into the reservoir at the back of the stove. A stove lid clanked off, sticks of wood scraped as they went in, the lid clanked back on. Less than five minutes later he panted to a halt at the bedroom door to find her perched on the edge of a wooden chair, back arched, eyes closed.

"Prudence!" He dropped to one knee before her.

"It's all right now," she said softly, and drew a deep breath as she ran her fingers through his hair.

His finger, quivering with fear, traced her chin. "Prudence, I'm so sorry I yelled at you. I didn't mean it. I'm so scared I can't think straight. I can't do this, Prudence. Isn't there time to get Kate?"

"I don't know, Jonathan, but please don't leave me alone. Please." Her eyes filled with pleading.

A crush of panic crowded in on him. He could barely remember his name. His hands shook, his eyes blurred, he couldn't catch his breath. And his stomach was doing strange things. In this condition what could he possibly do to help her? But he promised, "I won't leave you, not ever."

"You need to go downstairs and boil some scissors and some hard string."

To force his brain to function, he turned her instructions into a chant as he raced to the kitchen. Afraid something would happen while he wasn't at her side, he pumped the fire in the stove with bellows. But nothing he did seemed to hurry the water to a boil. He alternated between moaning with frustration and praying that a miracle would bring Kate home early. When he returned to the bedroom with the boiled items, she was lovingly cataloging each item of clothing for the baby—a tiny white flannel kimono, a flannel blanket, an undershirt, a diaper, and an incredibly small pair of blue booties. She turned and found him watching.

Her smile was so jubilant, so unafraid, it brought him a tiny measure of calm.

She looked deeply into his eyes and told him, "I'm awfully glad you're here, Jonathan."

"I'm glad I am, too." But it wasn't true at all. He wanted to be on a fast horse on his way into town to bring back Kate and a doctor. Instead he tried to appear calm and in control, excusing himself to go see to the fire in the kitchen stove and to be sure the reservoir and teakettle were full and hot.

When he returned, she was walking slowly along the hallway. "What are you doing now?"

"Come walk with me," she answered. "Kate says it helps move things along faster."

If it were up to him, he'd postpone things forever. He didn't think he could go through with this. Not with Prudence. Not when he loved her so much. And then he was ashamed of himself. If he weren't here for her, what would she do? How could he live with himself? So he held her in the crook of his arm and accompanied her as if they were strolling on the green on a Sunday afternoon. He teased her when she faltered, soothed when she fretted, listened when she needed to talk. And, every time they passed the window at the end of the hall, he looked for Kate.

"I think I'll lie down now," she said, at last. "I do believe it's time to scrub your hands."

The words hammered through him. *It's time. It's time. It's time. Time for his mother to die. Time for Anna to die. Time for Prudence to die.* He staggered blindly from the room and down the stairs into the kitchen. At the washstand, he scrubbed until his knuckles were raw, fighting down panic. He had never been this terrified in his life. He looked in the mirror. *Stop looking like you're at her funeral. You're not!* he ordered himself sharply. But his knees seemed made of sponge and the climb back upstairs endless.

The closer he came to the bed, the worse his hands trembled and he couldn't swallow the cotton filling his mouth. *You know how this is done. It's just like a cow having a calf, a dog having pups. Nature's the same when it comes to birthing.* That's what he told himself, but he didn't believe a word of it. He'd never seen a cow or a dog die in birthing. And he was all the help Prudence had, which was to say she was alone.

"Jonathan," she whispered.

"I'm here." He moved to the side of the bed and sat in the hard wooden chair. "How are you?"

"I hurt." But she smiled at him and cradled her stomach.

He tried to return the smile, but his face felt like a block of wood. He hunched his shoulders and sat in misery, waiting, feeling useless, helpless, terrified. When she held her breath, he held his. When her face contorted, so did his. When she bared her teeth, he bared his. But she never cried out. Not once. And all the while he found himself crooning words of love and devotion for her and silently, making extravagant promises to God if he would spare Prudence's life and give them a healthy baby.

Prudence's discomfort grew more intense as the pains came at more regular intervals, but she was conscious of little else but Jonathan. She clung to his hands and concentrated on the tenderness in his voice, filling herself with his love, rising above and out of the pain.

"Prudence, my darling, it's quite natural for a woman to yell at this time. It helps somehow, they tell me," Jonathan said softly, but her head thrashed from side to side in refusal.

As her need of him increased, Jonathan's fears disappeared. His churning insides grew calm. His hands steadied. His prayers for knowledge and ability poured out nonstop as the baby's birth grew closer to reality.

It was in the midst of just such a prayer that Prudence and Jonathan's daughter chose to make her appearance. Into his waiting hands spilled a tiny little girl, filling his heart with a wild throb of excitement, his face with a wide smile of delight.

"She's here, Darling, she's here, and she's a wonder." He held the baby close and Prudence reached out to touch the perfect little head, lifting her own with effort. She fell back into the pillows and laughed weakly while tears trickled down her temples.

"Is she pretty?" Prudence asked.

In her present state, she was certainly not what he would call pretty, but Prudence mustn't know that. "She's. . . she's wonderful."

Then, with no warning Prudence went limp.

Jonathan stood with the unwashed baby in his hands, paralyzed with terror at what he knew had happened. "God!" he screamed. "How could you do this to me a third time?" Such rage as Jonathan never believed possible filled him as he looked into Prudence's white face.

There was complete silence in the room, a silence broken by the click of the front door as it shut and the sound of feet easing up the stairs and along the hallway. Kate filled the open doorway, paused, then rushed to the bedside.

Jonathan, still holding the baby in outstretched hands, felt his blood run from glacial ice to molton lava. Tears blurred his vision. "She's dead!" He forced himself to say the words, though they choked him.

Kate took the baby and quickly examined her. "Neither 'she' is dead," Kate snapped, her voice rough from her effort to hold back her own emotions. She continued to work over the baby until there came a thin cry, not strong but thoroughly angry. "Your daughter's small, but she'll have good care. We'll see to that. She'll make it."

Jonathan looked from child to mother. He stared in horror at Prudence's waxy pale face and splayed body lying so still, like a broken doll. He didn't believe Kate. Any idiot could see Prudence was dead. Engulfing waves of despair broke over him and he staggered from the room.

Kate finished caring for Prudence then went in search of Jonathan. She found him in the room off the kitchen, slumped over Prudence's sewing machine, his shoulders still heaving with tired sobs. She wiped her own eyes, squared her shoulders, and brought him a wet towel.

"A fine one you are, Jonathan Hartwell! You stay firm as a rock through the worst of it, then fall apart. Now wipe your face and listen to me."

His bleary eyes focused on her. Meekly, he did as she ordered, concentrating closely on her words.

"First of all, Prudence has overworked and been under terrible mental stress. I believe that's what brought the baby early. But with rest and care, she'll be good as new.

"As for the baby, she's fine, too, and strong. She's fully formed and breathing normally. She'll need good care, but then what baby doesn't? You can't ask for more than the Lord's given you this day." Kate smiled at him. "Prudence'll sleep for some time now, but you're the one she'll want to see when she wakes. But, I promise I'll lock you out of the house if you wear that mourning face again."

Jonathan heard Kate's words, but he didn't trust them. He had seen Prudence. He knew the look of death. Why was Kate torturing him? "I wish I could believe you, Kate. With all my heart I want to believe that Prudence is alive, but I can still see her lying there, still as death."

"Since no words of mine will change your mind, give me a minute more and you can see for yourself."

Kate finally let Jonathan into Prudence's bedroom and led him to her bedside. Her face was alabaster, and dark lashes smudged pale cheeks, but there was a hint of pink on her lips and her breathing was deep and regular.

Jonathan dropped to his knees and buried his head in his hands. "Thank you, God," he breathed. "Thank you." He made no effort to stem the tide of tears that washed over his unshaven cheeks.

"All right, enough of that," Kate said, briskly. "There's someone waiting to look you over." She laid the baby in his arms. He looked hard at this baby, studying this daughter as he had not Serena, seeing her, really seeing her for the first time. She was very small, but she was perfectly formed from toes, to fingers, to the tiny shell curves of the ears, to the soft pulsing crown of her head. "I know you're going to make it, little one," he whispered, and his heart swelled with love for his second daughter. "You must, for your mother and Serena and me."

Kate took the baby, nestled her beside Prudence and left,

blinking back the threatening tears at the look of tenderness and love on the rugged logger's face.

Prudence opened her eyes to the same expression.

Jonathan had sat in a chair by the bed for hours, watching her sleep. He felt more peaceful than he ever had in his life. Though her face was pale and shadowed in the dim lamplight, he could already see that the lines of pain there from her struggle to give birth were vanishing. She looked so young. The women had dried and brushed her hair, and it spread in a golden brown fan across the pillow. Carefully, he touched a strand.

She woke and focused on him, and then he saw the look of fear beginning as her hand moved down to touch her now flat belly. He caught her hand before she could cry out. "Shhh, my love. We have a daughter, a small but very spunky daughter who's sound asleep beside you."

Tears of relief and joy filled Prudence's eyes as she turned to look at the baby. With her index finger, she caressed the dark curls. "Oh, Jonathan, she's beautiful, isn't she?" She raised questioning eyes to him.

"With such a beauty for a mother, she could be no less. Serena is going to be delirious with joy at having a little sister. Any thoughts for a name?"

Prudence hesitated and gathered her forces. "If it suits you, I'd like to call her Anna Evangeline." She held her breath as she studied his reaction.

"A perfect name," he replied softly. "Anna would be so thrilled." Then, he bent over and looked deeply into her eyes filled with love for him, for them. "I do love you with all my heart, Prudence Beck Hartwell," Jonathan said softly, his voice husky with emotion. Then he kissed her soundly. "May God bless us, one and all."

Summer Dreams

*Four all-new inspirational novellas with
all the romance of a summer's day.*

Summer Breezes by Veda Boyd Jones
Law school graduate Melina Howard takes on Blake Allen, a
former sailing instructor, as her crew in a local regatta.

À la Mode by Yvonne Lehman
Small town florist Heather Willis is intrigued when she makes
the acquaintance of a mysterious stranger with a Texan accent.

King of Hearts by Tracie Peterson
Elise Jost is a non-traditional student whose life's direction takes
a different course when she makes a high grade with professor
Ian Hunter.

No Groom for the Wedding by Kathleen Yapp
A professional photographer, Penny Blake is capturing her sister's honeymoon on film when she finds herself the focus of a
fellow cruise passenger.

352 pages, Paperbound, 5" x 8"
ONLY $4.97 for all four!

WHEN I'M ON MY KNEES

Anita Corrine Donihue

A beautiful compilation of prayers especially for women, prayers that emanate from the heart, prayers that deal with friendship, family, peace and praise. Packaged in a beautifully printed leatherette cover, women will also find hymns and poems that focus on the importance of prayer in their everyday lives. 212 pages, Printed leatherette, 4" x 6 ¾".

ONLY $4.97 each!

About the author:
Anita Corrine Donihue, a teacher with thirty years of experience, is the coauthor of *Apples for a Teacher* and *Joy to the World*, two very popular titles from Barbour Books.
